JACQUELINE WOODSON

feathers

PUFFIN BOOKS

PUFFIN BOOKS
Published by the Penguin Group

Penguin Young Readers Group, 345 Hudson Street, New York, New York 10014, U.S.A.
Penguin Group (Canada), 90 Eglinton Avenue East, Suite 700,
Toronto, Ontario, Canada M4P 2Y3 (a division of Pearson Penguin Canada Inc.)
Penguin Books Ltd, 80 Strand, London WC2R 0RL, England
Penguin Ireland, 25 St Stephen's Green, Dublin 2, Ireland (a division of Penguin Books Ltd)
Penguin Group (Australia), 250 Camberwell Road, Camberwell, Victoria 3124, Australia
(a division of Pearson Australia Group Pty Ltd)
Penguin Books India Pvt Ltd, 11 Community Centre,
Panchsheel Park, New Delhi - 110 017, India
Penguin Group (NZ), 67 Apollo Drive, Rosedale, North Shore 0632, New Zealand
(a division of Pearson New Zealand Ltd)
Penguin Books (South Africa) (Pty) Ltd, 24 Sturdee Avenue,
Rosebank, Johannesburg 2196, South Africa

Registered Offices: Penguin Books Ltd, 80 Strand, London WC2R 0RL, England

First published in the United States of America by G. P. Putnam's Sons,
a division of Penguin Young Readers Group, 2007
Published by Puffin Books, a division of Penguin Young Readers Group, 2009

3 5 7 9 10 8 6 4

THE LIBRARY OF CONGRESS HAS CATALOGED THE G. P. PUTNAM'S SONS EDITION AS FOLLOWS:
Woodson, Jacqueline.
Feathers / Jacqueline Woodson.
p.   cm.
Summary: When a new, white student nicknamed "The Jesus Boy" joins her
sixth grade class in the winter of 1971, Frannie's growing friendship with him
makes her start to see some things in a new light.
ISBN: 978-0-399-23989-2 (hc)
[1. Race relations—Fiction. 2. African Americans—Fiction. 3. Schools—Fiction. 4. Deaf—
Fiction. 5. Family life—Fiction. 6. Religion—Fiction.]
I. Title
PZ7.W868Fe 2007
[Fic]—dc22   2006024713

Puffin Books ISBN 978-0-14-241198-8

Printed in the United States of America

for Juliet

Hope is the thing with feathers
that perches in the soul,
And sings the tune—without the words,
And never stops at all
            —EMILY DICKINSON

PART ONE

1

His coming into our classroom that morning was the only new thing. Everything else was the same way it'd always been. The snow coming down. Ms. Johnson looking out the window, then after a moment, nodding. The class cheering because she was going to let us go out into the school yard at lunchtime.

It had been that way for days and days.

And then, just before the lunch bell rang, he walked into our classroom.

Stepped through that door white and softly as the snow.

The class got quiet and the boy reached into his pocket and pulled something out. *A note for you, Ms. Johnson,* the boy said. And the way his voice sounded, all new and soft in the room, made most of the class laugh out loud.

But Ms. Johnson gave us a look and the class got quiet.

Now isn't this the strangest thing, I thought, watching the boy.

Just that morning I'd been thinking about the year I'd missed a whole month of school, showing up in late October after everybody had already buddied up. I'd woken up with that thought and, all morning long, hadn't been able to shake it.

The boy was pale and his hair was long—almost to his back. And curly—like my own brother's hair but Mama would *never* let Sean's hair grow that long. I sat at my desk, staring at his hair, wondering what a kid like that was doing in our school—with that long, curly hair and white skin and all.

And he was skinny too. Tall and skinny with white, white hands hanging down below his coat sleeves. Skinny white neck showing above his collar. Brown corduroy bell-bottoms like the ones I was wearing. Not a pair of gloves in sight, just a beat-up dark green book bag that looked like it had a million things in it hanging heavy from his shoulder.

Ms. Johnson said, "Welcome to our sixth-grade classroom," and the boy looked up at her and smiled.

Trevor was sitting in the row in front of me, and when the boy smiled, he coughed but the cough was trying to cover up a word that we weren't allowed to say. Ms. Johnson shot him a look and Trevor just shrugged and tapped his pencil on his desk like he was tapping out a beat in his head. The boy looked at Trevor and Trevor coughed the word again but softer this time. Still, Ms. Johnson heard it.

"You have one more chance, Mr. Trevor," Ms. Johnson said, opening her attendance book and writing something in it with her red pen. Trevor glared at the boy but didn't say the word again. The boy stared back at him—his face pale and calm and quiet. I had never seen such a calm look on a kid. Grown-ups could look that way sometimes, but not the kids I knew. The boy's eyes moved slowly around the classroom but his head stayed still. It felt like he was seeing all of us, taking us in and figuring us out. When his eyes got to me, I made a face, but he just smiled a tiny, calm smile and then his eyes moved on.

I looked down at my notebook. Beneath my name, I had written the date—Wednesday, January 6, 1971. The day before, Ms. Johnson had read us a poem about hope getting inside you and never stopping. I had written that part of the poem down—*Hope is the thing with feathers*—because I had loved the sound of it. Loved the way the words seemed to float across my notebook.

When I told Mama about the poem, she'd said, *Welcome to the seventies, Frannie. Sounds like Ms. Johnson's trying to tell you all something about looking forward instead of back all the time.* I just stared at Mama. The poem was about *hope* and how hope had these feathers on it. It didn't have a single thing to do with looking forward or back or even *sideways.* But then Sean came home and I told him about the poem and the crazy thing Mama had said. Sean smiled and shook his head. *You're a fool,* he signed to me. *The word* doesn't have feathers. It's a metaphor. *Don't you learn anything at Price?*

So maybe the seventies is the thing with feathers. Maybe it was about hope and moving forward and not looking behind you. Some days, I tried to understand all that grown-up stuff. But a lot of it still didn't make any sense to me.

When I looked up from my notebook, Ms. Johnson had assigned the boy a seat close to the front of the room, and when he sat down, I heard him let out a sigh.

Something about the way the new boy sat there, with his shoulders all slumped and his head bent down, made me blink hard. The sadness came on fast. I tried to think of something different, the Christmas that had just passed and the presents I'd gotten. Mama's face when Daddy leaned across the couch to hug her tight. My older brother, Sean, holding up a basketball jersey and signing, *I forgot I told you I wanted this!* His face all broken out into a grin, his hands flying through the air. I put the picture of the sign for *forgot* in my head—four fingers sliding across the forehead like they're wiping away a thought. Sometimes the signs took me to a different thinking place.

The bell rang and Ms. Johnson said, "I'll do a formal introduction after lunch."

All of us got up at the same time and stood in two straight lines, girls on one side, boys on the other. Ms. Johnson led us out of the classroom and down the hall toward the cafeteria. As usual, Rayray acted the fool, doing some crazy dance steps and a quick half-split when Ms. Johnson wasn't looking.

Trevor turned to the boy and whispered, "Don't no pale-faces go to this school. You need to get your white butt back across the highway."

"I know I don't hear anyone talking behind me," Ms. Johnson said before the boy could say anything back. But the boy just stared at Trevor as we walked. Even after, when Trevor turned back around, the boy continued looking.

"Face forward, Frannie," Ms. Johnson said. I turned forward.

"You're just as pale as I am . . . my brother," I heard the boy say.

When I turned around again, the boy was looking at Trevor, his face still calm even though the words he'd just spoken were hanging in the air.

Trevor took a deep breath, but before he could turn around again, Ms. Johnson did. She looked at the boy and raised her eyebrows.

"We don't talk while we're on line," she said. "Do we?"

"No, Ms. Johnson," the whole class said.

When Rayray saw how mad Trevor was getting, he looked scared. When he saw me watching him, he pointed to the boy and pulled his finger across his neck.

"If I have to ask you to turn around again, Frannie, I'm pulling you up here with me."

I faced forward again.

Trevor was light, lighter than most of the other kids who went to our school, and blue-eyed. On the first day of school, Rayray made the mistake of asking him if he was part white and Trevor hit him. Hard. After that, nobody asked that question anymore. But I had heard Mama and a neighbor talking about Trevor's daddy, how he was a white man who lived across the highway. And for a while, there were lots of kids at school whispering. But nobody said anything to Trevor. As the months passed and he kept getting in trouble for hitting people, we figured out that he had a mean streak in him—one minute he'd be smiling, the next his blue eyes would get all small and he'd be ramming himself into somebody who'd said the wrong thing or given him the wrong look. Sometimes, he'd just sneak up behind a person and slap the back of their head—for no reason. The whole class was a little bit afraid of him, but Rayray was *a lot* afraid.

As we walked down the hall, I stared at Trevor's back, wondering how long the boy would have to wait before he got his head slapped.

2

I could smell burgers and French fries in the cafeteria. Mr. Hungry was hollering loud in my stomach, so I didn't think anything else about the boy until he showed up on the lunch line in front of me. I watched him take a fish sandwich, French fries and chocolate pudding. The fish sandwiches were for the kids that didn't like burgers and usually, at the end of lunch period, there were a whole lot of fish sandwiches left. I wrinkled my nose at his tray and tried to grab two burgers.

"You know the rules, Frannie," Miss Costa, the lunch lady, said. "Come back when you're done with the first one."

"I was just trying to save myself a trip," I said, putting a burger back.

The boy looked over his shoulder and smiled at me again. Then he went and sat over in the corner, under the loudspeaker.

I sat down across from Maribel Tanks only because it was right next to Samantha.

"Have you lost your mind," I whispered to Samantha.

Samantha just looked at me with one of her eyebrows raised and I knew she was thinking what she was always saying, which was *I'm not the one that doesn't like Maribel—that's you.*

Me and Samantha went back to first grade together. One

day, I was just this little kid alone in the first grade, coming into class a month after everyone. For a whole week, I didn't have a single friend. And then, the next week, there was Samantha walking over to me, saying, "Do you want to play?" Even though we weren't the kind of friends that always spent every single second together and dressed alike and stuff like that, we hung real tight at school.

Me and Maribel *never* played. We hardly even talked. She had gone to private school and then, in fourth grade, that school closed, and since her parents didn't want to send her across the highway for private school, she came to Price. But, to hear her tell it, you'd think she was still in some high and mighty private school—always finding some kind of way to drop it into a conversation, always wrinkling her nose at me like she couldn't even believe we had to share the same air.

I looked over at the boy. He had his head bent over his food like he was praying.

"I can't believe this nasty lunch costs money," Maribel was saying. She took a loud sip of milk, then stirred it around with her straw like it was some kind of special drink. "When I was at the Casey School, we could bring our own lunch or eat the lunch the school made. And that lunch was always delicious."

I gave Samantha a look but she wouldn't give me a look back.

Everybody at our school got lunch for free except Maribel Tanks—but my mama said that was just Maribel's mama putting on airs. Maribel's mama owned Tanks Groceries, but we didn't shop there because the prices were way too high. Even for things like eggs, which should have cost regular everywhere—at Tanks they cost twenty cents more and Mama said that's twenty cents more than what she was gonna pay for them. She said those high prices were just more Tanks putting on airs. Mama said one day the Tanks were gonna go put on so many airs they'd just up and float away. I don't know about all that, but when Mama got to talking about people, I liked to listen. My grandmother always said Mama had the gift of gab and that I inherited it. I didn't know about all that either. I though of myself as more of a listener than a talker. Except with stuff like math and science and geography. Then I'm a starer-out-the-window kind of person.

Maribel took another loud sip and turned to look at the boy. He was sitting by himself at the end of a table, just looking down at his tray as he stuffed food into his mouth. The sadness tried to creep back up in me, so I started talking real fast to push it down again.

"You'd think they'd assign him a partner or something," I said.

"Like who," Maribel said. *"You?"*

"No! Like another boy or something. That doesn't even make sense, him sitting by himself like that. All new and everything."

Samantha nodded.

"Then go sit with him," Maribel said. "Go be a Good Samaritan. We collected coats at the store for poor kids—that's my good deed for the year." She looked over at the boy again. "That coat he's wearing looks like one of the ones we gave out too. Don't know why he's wearing it in this hot lunchroom, though."

"Oh, hush the hole in your head already." I took another bite of burger and glared at her while I chewed.

"Well, at least I only got *one* hole in my head," she said. Samantha smiled at that even though it wasn't even a tiny bit funny.

"He came into the store yesterday," Maribel said. "By himself. Maybe he likes it that way. And he bought a ham and cheese hero with extra mayo, some cupcakes and a soda, that's all. And then when he paid for it, he used mostly pennies. That made my mama so mad!"

"What's wrong with pennies," I said, taking another big bite before even swallowing all of the last one. "Pennies are money like anything else."

Maribel sighed—one of those trying-to-sound-like-a-grown-up sounds. "Oh Frannie."

That's all. Just *Oh Frannie*. With all that air around it.

" 'Oh Frannie' nothing. Pennies are money. Oh Maribel Tanks."

Maribel just rolled her eyes at me, then let them slide back over to the boy.

"Pennies *are* money," Samantha said. "You got a hundred, you got a dollar."

"Yeah," Maribel said. "Try counting out *two hundred and ten* of them. And have your hands stinking with that old sweaty penny smell." She made a face, wiping her hand against her shirt like the smell was still on it. "Anyway, it's strange—you don't see white boys at this school. Much as I hate to say it, Trevor's right—that boy belongs across the highway with the other white people."

"It's the nineteen seventies," I said. "Not the fifties. There's no more segregation, remember?"

"Try telling that to the people on the other side of the highway," Maribel said. "Or the people on this side. It's strange. Strange that he's coming to this side where he doesn't belong."

It *was* strange, but I wasn't going to agree with Maribel about it.

"Who belongs anywhere?" Samantha said. She unfolded a tissue to blow her nose. When she blew it, she leaned down and away from the table like I wouldn't have thought of doing. She even excused herself afterward. "I mean," she said, sitting back up and tucking the tissue all delicate-like into her bag, "he belongs where he belongs. If he ended up here, then that's where he belongs."

Maribel rolled her eyes again. "Well, if he comes into my store with those pennies again, I'm not taking them. He better go find some *dollars* somewhere." Maribel's hair was straightened and curled under, hanging down her back and over her shoulders. She ran her fingers through it while she stared at the boy, her eyebrows bent all out of shape.

Maribel was Rayray's cousin on his daddy's side, but the only resemblance between them was they both had really smooth brown skin. My own skin was dark brown too, but it wasn't all smooth and pretty like Rayray's and Maribel's. It was just regular. Like my hair. Mama had tried to put some heat to it to straighten out the kink just once. When I looked in the mirror after she'd done it, I felt like a stranger to myself. After that, I just let my hair do what it wanted to do and mostly kept it in braids. Once in a while, I'd pick it out into an Afro like the teenagers wore, but if Mama saw it that way, she snatched it right back into a braid, telling me if I wanted to wear my hair like a teenager, I needed to *be* a teenager. Sometimes she didn't make the least bit of sense. The Afro pick had a red, black and green Black Power fist on it. Mostly I just kept it in my back pocket with the fist sticking out. That was the way a lot of kids carried their Afro picks. Mama frowned when she saw it.

"It's not *your* store," I said. "It's your mama's."

"It's *my* inheritance."

I guess that's better than inheriting a gab gift, but I didn't say anything. After that, we ate mostly without doing a whole lot of talking about the boy.

Samantha ate her food delicately, all ladylike. Every way that she was ladylike, I wasn't. I looked down at my turtle-neck—it was light blue, but a big drop of greasy ketchup had spilled on it. I took a deep breath. Sometimes, I wished Samantha and me could trade places and I could see what it felt like to be like her, to be all delicate and careful and sure like that.

I moved a little bit closer to her, pulled my napkin off my tray and wiped at the stain. It just smeared to a light brown. Maribel looked at the spot, made a face and looked away.

Later on, when we were all out in the school yard, me and Samantha split a chocolate cupcake. Just as we were finishing up, standing there licking the frosting off of our fingers, Rayray, Trevor, Chris and some other guys went over to the boy. He was sitting on the ground with his arms wrapped around his knees, not even caring that the ground was all wet. He had on dark brown boots and was kicking his heel into the snow, just minding his own business.

"What's your name anyway," Rayray said.

And the boy looked at him—kind of squinty-eyed—like a million things were going on inside his own head that were miles and miles away from all of us. When I was a baby, Mama said old people would look at me and say, "Oh Lord, this child's got an old spirit. She's been here before." *It was the way you looked at everyone and everything,* Mama said. *Like you were taking every little bit and piece of it in.* I'd never really understood what they were talking about until now.

"My *boy* Rayray asked you your name," Trevor said. "You deaf or something?" Rayray started hitting at his own ears and making strange mumbling sounds.

I flinched a little bit. It was no good when people said things like *you deaf or something.* My brother was deaf and deaf *was* something.

I leaned against the school yard fence with Samantha, both of us watching but neither of us saying anything. Samantha took a napkin from her bag and rubbed the last of the frosting from her fingers. She offered it to me but I just held out my hand, showing her how clean I'd licked it.

Most days, I broke away from the fence and went and jumped rope or played handball with other kids. But Samantha was always by the fence when I returned. Sometimes, she was bent over her tiny Bible. I could see Maribel out in the school yard, doing "Down, Down Baby" with three other girls.

Down, down baby
Down by the rollercoaster
Sweet, sweet baby I will never let you go,
Jimmy, jimmy coco-pop. Jimmy jimmy pow!
I know a lady . . .

Maribel's hand went the wrong way and she was out. I couldn't help smiling. When I looked back, Trevor was still talking junk.

The sign for *believe* flashed into my head—the way Sean signed it—his pointer finger against the side of his head like he's saying "think," then his hands coming together—like the sign for *marry*. I stood there thinking, for the first time, about how perfect that word was—to have a thought in your head and then to marry it, to take it into your heart forever . . .

"I can't believe Trevor's still messing with that boy," I whispered, hoping I hadn't just made the sign. Sometimes I did that, talked to myself in sign language.

Rayray made some stupid fake signs with his hands, then grunted. "I guess we gotta talk to him like a deaf guy, huh?" he said. The other boys laughed. But when Rayray looked over and saw me watching, he stopped, put his hands in his pockets and got quiet.

The boy just looked up at all of them. Then he did something amazing. He took his hands out of his pocket and signed, *No, I'm not deaf.* Then he looked over at me and smiled—like he'd known all along I was standing over by the fence, watching him. I looked away real fast, hoping he hadn't seen the surprise on my face.

"Are those real signs?" Samantha asked me. "Or is he just being jive and faking it?"

"It's real," I said. "He's saying he's not deaf, that's all."

"Well, how does he know that?"

"How am I supposed to know? I don't know that boy!"

Maribel had come back over to the fence and was standing on the other side of Samantha. "It's not like you have to be a *genius* or something to know some signs," she said.

But Samantha looked at the boy like she was seeing something new and magical in him.

"You look like Jesus," Trevor said. Then he kicked the boy's boot and said, "You better learn how to answer a soul brother when they be talking to you, Jesus Boy."

"He *does* look like Jesus," Samantha said slowly.

"Kind of, I guess," Maribel said. "There used to be this boy at the Casey School who looked like Michael Jackson. But he couldn't even dance."

I rolled my eyes. "Maribel Tanks. If you didn't have a neck, your head would just float away."

Samantha smiled but she didn't take her eyes off the Jesus Boy.

He was looking down at the ground. After a few minutes, he lifted his head a little bit and stared calmly past everything and everybody—his lips pressed together, his hair lifting up in the wind. I tried to see all the things he was seeing. But all I saw was the highway out past the school yard. A tiny dot of an airplane. The sun slipping back behind some clouds. And miles and miles of wet, gray sky.

3

Imagine, my brother signed. *Imagine if somebody built a bridge right outside our window and we could just walk across the highway and be on the other side.*

We were sitting together on the window seat, staring out at the wet snow, the gray sky and the cars moving along the highway—tiny and slow in the distance. I was thinking about the Jesus Boy. There weren't white people on this side of the highway. You didn't notice until one appeared. And then you saw all the brown and light brown everywhere. And then you started to wonder. The first time I asked Mama about it, she said, *They don't want to live over here.* And the way she said it made me wonder what was so wrong with *our* side of the highway.

Why would we want to cross the highway, anyway? I asked Sean. *What would we want to see?*

What wouldn't you want to see? Sean said.

I wish I could explain the sign for *what.* With sign language, there are different ways of moving your face and hands for the same word. Like there's *what* that means "Shut up, kid, you're bothering me." And there's *what* that's "really interested in what somebody wants to say to you." You do sort of the same thing with your hands, but your face does other stuff.

I like this side, I said.

Sean kept staring out the window.

Maybe if you were standing somewhere else and looking over here, you'd think the houses weren't real special. The way some of them could use new windows or some new paint. The way the doors hung off of some and other ones had some cardboard sometimes where a window should be.

Or maybe you'd see our apartment building and wonder about the names written on it or the way, just outside the fifth floor, someone's laundry had frozen on the line.

It was snowing hard again. I lifted the window a bit and stuck my hand out, caught some flakes in it and licked them off. Sean shivered and pulled the window closed.

You're crazy, he said.

What's wrong with walking down to the overpass?

If you wanted to cross the highway from where we lived, you had to pray first. Then you had to run real fast. Or you could walk a half mile down and then there's an overpass that takes you to that other side. Either way, it was a lot of trouble.

It's different, Sean said. *I mean, like imagine if there was a bridge from every single window in the world to some whole new place. That would be crazy, wouldn't it? It would mean we could all just step out of our worlds into these whole new ones.*

I shook my head. *It's fine here. It's beautiful.*

It *was* beautiful. Somebody had written some names on our building, and even though all the grown-ups complained about it and tried to wash them off, I secretly loved the bright colors of the spray paint—the way the names looked super-big written out like that—like some giant had come along with

17

giant markers. And when I looked at the windows that had pieces of cardboard trying to fill in the places where the glass should be, I thought about the way the sun had to climb over and through the spaces where the cardboard wasn't to sneak into that house. And when the sun found its way through, I figured it left these beautiful bright yellow lines over everything inside.

We had everything we needed on this side—huge supermarkets like Bohack when you have to do the big family shop once a week, tiny old Tanks store when you were last-minute desperate for something like high-priced milk. We had the Price School, where I went—Mama said we could make-believe it was named for Leontyne Price, the black opera singer, but it's really named for Major Price, the white mayor from a long time ago—and the Daffodil School, where Sean went. The Daffodil School's for kids who don't learn like other kids. Like Sean. He can't hear, so you have to use sign language with him. He can talk a little bit, but most people don't understand what he's saying. I guess that's because you have to listen real hard and most people don't want to spend a lot of energy on listening to people. Across the highway, there's another school like Sean's called Starship Academy. Mama said even if we lived on that side of the highway, she'd cross it every day to come to the Daffodil School because there was no way on God's green earth she'd send Sean to a school that sounded like it was for people from outer space. There's a regular school over there called Eastbay. You always saw cars on the highway that said MY CHILD'S AN HONOR STUDENT AT EASTBAY, which was basically another way of saying I LIVE ON

THE WHITE SIDE OF THE HIGHWAY. Price had those bumper stickers too. Samantha had gotten a couple of them, and once she even gave me one, but Daddy said maybe we should wait until I actually *was* an honor student before he put it on his bumper.

On our side of the highway we also have a library. Mama calls the library "the day care center" because most of the kids in there are waiting for their parents to get home from work. There's a real day care center called Little Sprouts and one for kids with things different about them called Special Little Sprouts. Both of them got flowers and little hands painted on the windows, and some days, if it was raining or just real cloudy, I walked by and saw those flowers and those tiny little painted hands and it filled me with such an emptiness. Some days, it felt like the times when I got to make handprints and flowers and stuff just slipped away from me before I even got a chance to figure out how much fun being a little kid was. Seems the minute I turned around, I was already more than eleven years old.

Some days, eleven felt like a whole long lifetime. All heavy like that.

If somebody did build that bridge, Sean, I said, *who do you think would be the first to cross it? Somebody from that side? Or somebody from our side?*

I'd cross it, Sean said. *I don't mind being the first.*

And then what?

I don't know. Sean shrugged and kept staring out the window, his eyes getting that faraway look. His hands quiet on the sill.

4

On the second day after the Jesus Boy got to our school, Trevor was absent and Rayray said it was because he broke his arm. Then everybody wanted to know how, crowding around Rayray to be the first ones to get the information.

"He missed the fence," Rayray said. "He was tryna jump from the big swings to this high fence that's like three feet away and he wasn't swinging high enough. I *told* that jive turkey before he even jumped that he needed to be swinging higher than that because even a fool knows you gotta get some height to fly over to the fence! When his mama was taking him to the emergency room, she said, 'If your arm isn't broken, *I'm* gonna break it because I told you about jumping out of those swings like that.'"

Everybody laughed, but it was hard for me not to imagine Trevor falling through the air—how scared he must have been, reaching and grabbing at nothing. I turned and looked at Samantha. She was shaking her head but maybe she was thinking the same thing.

In the summertime, Trevor's skin turned the prettiest copper brown. Once, when he was standing next to me at the park, I saw his bare arms up close, just hanging all quiet along his sides—and the skin, the way it had so many beautiful colors in it, the way it looked all golden somehow, stopped me. I stared at his arms and saw the Trevor that was maybe inside of the Evil Trevor—just a regular boy with beautiful skin. I saw that, even though he was mean all the time, the sun still stopped and colored him and warmed him—like it did to everybody else.

When I got to my desk, I looked up and saw the Jesus Boy looking at me. I couldn't tell what his face was trying to say— it was just blank and open and strange. I cut my eyes at him and opened my notebook even though I didn't have to yet.

Maribel's seat was right behind mine.

"That Jesus Boy is always *looking* at you," she whispered.

"Only way you'd know is if you're always looking at *him*," I whispered back. I felt her poke me in the back, but ignored it.

I wrote my name at the top of the page. Beneath it, I wrote the date. Beneath that, I drew a picture of a kid on a swing. Kids said it felt like flying to jump through the air, catch onto that fence, then let yourself climb down. They said something about being up that high let you see all over the place in a way that felt different than looking at the world from a window. I thought back to the day before when me and Sean were talking about those bridges he wanted built. Seems kids on this side of the highway were always trying to figure out ways to fly and run and cross over things and . . . get free or something.

Maribel was wearing a green sweater with THE CASEY SCHOOL written across the front in white letters. The sweater was too small and there were tiny lint balls on it. Everybody always seemed to be thinking about some other place.

I snuck another look at the Boy. He was still staring at me. I stuck out my tongue at him and turned to a clean page.

Ms. Johnson came in, took attendance and then she said, "Did everyone get a chance to personally introduce themselves to . . ." And then she said the new boy's name again—like she'd done the day before.

But I don't remember it now because the minute she called it, he stood up and said, "Everybody calls me Jesus, Ms. Johnson." Some of the kids laughed. Most of us just looked at him.

Ms. Johnson looked around at all of us and all of us found other stuff besides her to look at.

"I like Jesus," the boy said and sat back down.

I don't know if he meant he liked Jesus the person or Jesus the name, but I guess Ms. Johnson thought it was Jesus the name because she said, "Okay . . . Jesus." Her face just stayed calm so we couldn't tell what she was thinking.

"There's only two things wrong with that," Rayray said. He was sitting way in the back of the classroom and everybody turned around real fast to look at him. For a minute, the only sound was chair legs scraping against the floor.

"What's that?" Ms. Johnson said. She was frowning now. Ms. Johnson's a good teacher in a lot of ways. She laughs and I like teachers who laugh. And once a week she brings some kinda snack for us all—like doughnuts or mini candy bars or cinnamon graham crackers or really sweet cherries. And she always seems to bring the snacks on a day when I'm the hungriest, which is usually a day when school lunch is the worst—like on goulash day when they pour this stewy stuff that has things like green peppers and eggplant in it all over perfectly good rice and completely ruin it. Whenever they have that, I ask if I could just have the rice and Miss Costa always says *No* like it's against some kind of school-lunch law to serve goulash and rice separately. So on those days I'm really hungry and that's usually when Ms. Johnson decides to pull out her snacks.

The other nice thing about Ms. Johnson is she wants you to understand stuff. I mean, she doesn't just teach us and if we don't get it, she keeps on moving. She really cares about us understanding things and she'll take a real long time explaining something until she's sure everybody's got it. Sometimes that's a little bit boring if you already understand it and she's still explaining it. But that doesn't happen with me because I'm usually the last one to get it. The things I don't understand the most are science, math, grammar and geography. I understand independent reading and journal time and I understand the story part of writing but not things like diagramming a sentence or semicolons. Anyway, that's why when Rayray said what he said, Ms. Johnson stopped taking attendance to ask him about it. She wanted herself and all of us to understand.

"What are the two things wrong with it, Rayray?" And that's another thing I like about Ms. Johnson—Rayray's name is really Raymond Raysen, but he decided he wanted everyone to call him Rayray. When he told Ms. Johnson that, she jumped right into calling him the name he wanted. Everybody calls me Frannie and so does Ms. Johnson, but even if I would've said, "Call me Floyjoy McCoy from now on, Ms. Johnson," my name would be Floyjoy McCoy. I guess it's

23

strange that nobody ever calls me by my first name—Abigail or even Abby. I guess it's because Sean can almost say Frannie—it sounds kind of crooked, like somebody saying it underwater, but we know what he's saying. And maybe that's why it stuck—because of him.

Rayray leaned back in his chair. He was wearing this big shirt that said BLACK IS BEAUTIFUL with a black hand making a Black Power fist underneath the words. The shirt was too big for Rayray. He's real skinny, so when he wears big clothes, mostly you see the clothes, not Rayray. He slouched down in his seat and just about disappeared into that big shirt.

"Well, first of all," he said, "Jesus wasn't a boy, he was like God's son but not a man either—like a *Thing*-type person. Like a spirit guy."

Ms. Johnson and the rest of us just looked at him.

"And second of all, he wasn't white. He was like spirit-colored or something."

"What's spirit-colored?" his friend Chris asked. "I never heard of no spirit color."

I could see Rayray's little head inside his big shirt. He was frowning. "Like the color of air, brother-man. You know, like no color."

"When those cats put nails in him, he bled, though," somebody else said. "What color was his blood?"

Rayray shrugged. "Right on, my brother-man, I feel what you're saying. Blood is red no matter who it's coming out of. But that ain't where I'm going, you see? That kid ain't Jesus is all *I'm* saying."

"Say, brother," the kid said, which was jive talk for *I agree with you.*

Say, brother, I signed underneath my desk, then looked down at my hands. I had a pockmark on the center of each palm left over from the time I had the chicken pox. The marks were small and reddish brown. Sometimes when I was thinking about something real hard, they started itching. Maybe in another world, somebody would've thought they were nail holes, I don't know.

Mama lost one baby before I was born. Her name was Lila and she died when she was a month old. Something about her lungs. Something about her blood. We don't talk about her much. But there are pictures. Sometimes Mama kisses my palms and calls me God's gift.

I wondered what the inside of the Jesus Boy's hands looked like. I wondered if his mama kissed them and called him silly names. Of course when I looked up, he was staring at me again. Old Big Eyes.

"He's not saying he's Jesus-Jesus, right?" Rayray asked. "He's saying that's—like some nickname. I know this Spanish guy named Jesus but it's pronounced the Spanish way—not like the real guy. This kid ain't saying he's the real guy, right? I mean, how's he gonna be God's son and be in Ms. Johnson's class? No offense, Ms. Johnson, but even if that Jesus Boy was spirit-colored, he wouldn't be coming to Price. If he was really God's son, he'd probably go to a private school."

"Like where?" Maribel said. "The Casey School closed.

There's not any private schools on this side of the highway. If there was one, I'd be going to it."

"Or like Catholic school," somebody else said. "Someplace with some religion, right?"

I saw Ms. Johnson smile a little bit. "I don't think that's what Jesus is saying about himself, everyone, are you?"

Ms. Johnson and everybody else looked at the Jesus Boy. He didn't move or shake his head or anything, just sat there, staring off.

"Are *you*?" Rayray asked him. "You aren't saying you're like God's son, are you?"

"I don't think it matters," Ms. Johnson said. "What matters is—"

"Aren't we all God's children?" Samantha said quietly. She looked around the room, taking us all in. "Each of you," she said, "is a true child of God." She turned to the Jesus Boy. "Maybe some are truer than others."

Rayray just looked at her and shrugged. "Jesus don't belong in this room is all I'm saying. And that cat's saying he's Je—" He stopped talking and stared at the Jesus Boy and frowned. Then we all looked at him.

He had his hands on his desk and was looking down at them. I saw a tear fall onto his pale hand and then another one, but he wiped them away real quick.

I heard myself saying, "He's crying, Ms. Johnson. The Jesus Boy is crying."

"Dag," Rayray said. "I didn't mean to make him cry. I swear, Ms. Johnson. I wasn't trying to be mean. I was just saying—"

"I'm not *crying*," Jesus Boy said real fast, shooting me a look that was so evil, I couldn't believe it came from his face.

"Are you all right?" Ms. Johnson said, her hand on his shoulder.

"Yeah. I'm okay," the Jesus Boy said, his voice soft again, so soft that maybe some of the kids didn't hear him.

"I lived on the other side of the highway already," the Jesus Boy said softly. He kept looking down at his hands, like he was talking to them, like he was talking to himself. "We . . . my family didn't belong there." He looked up and around at each one of us. It felt like everything stopped. There weren't tears in his eyes, but they were sad. "My daddy said it would be better here," he said, almost whispering it. "He said people would be . . . he said people would be . . . you know, nice to me." He looked down at his hands again. After a minute, he put his head down on his desk and sighed.

We all stared at him, and Ms. Johnson bent down and whispered something in his ear. He nodded and she put her hand on his back and led him out of the room. As he walked out the door, I could see that his face was all squinched up but his hands were just flat and calm, hanging down at his sides. Then he sniffed and his face just sort of sagged. I put my head down on my desk and closed my eyes.

"Is he some kind of crybaby or something?" I heard someone ask.

"Nah," I heard Rayray say softly. "You heard the brotherman. He's just like a little bit lost. It be's like that sometimes."

"Right on," I heard somebody else say. "It be's like that."

Usually, when Ms. Johnson left the room, we lost our

minds with talking and jumping around and throwing things at each other. Rayray always acted the craziest. He could do standing backflips and usually did them in the aisle. But that day, he just sat quietly in his seat, rolling his pencil slowly back and forth across his desk. That day, the room was completely quiet. It was like we were all glued to our seats. It was like somebody had come into the room and gently lifted our tongues right on out of our mouths.

PART TWO

5

When Mama's first baby died, she and my daddy started going to a small church around the corner from our house. She said the first time she sat down in that church, all this beautiful light came pouring in through the one stained-glass window above where the pastor stood. Mama said she watched the light and the light had so many things in it— color and dust, hard and soft patches of sun. She said she sat there and leaned into that light and it warmed her and helped her understand. *And what I understood,* Mama said, *was that the baby would always be with us—somewhere, somehow. When we needed her.*

They had named the baby girl Lila, after my mother's great-grandmother. Mama says she saw Lila in that light, reaching out a tiny brown baby hand to her and smiling.

I don't know if I believe in miracles. I think things happen and we need to believe in them. But sometimes, out of the corner of my eye, I'll catch Lila smiling at me, her head covered with jet-black curls, her lips curling up over her tiny toothless mouth, her tiny hands reaching.

6

At the corner of North Conduit and Eastbay Road, there's a little stream that gets deeper when there's a lot of rain or snow. In the winter, the thinnest sheet of ice freezes over it and there's always a rainbow bouncing off that ice.

Me and Samantha walked down North Conduit the way we'd done for as long as I could remember. The only thing different about it all was how quiet we were. Samantha stared down at the snow, taking careful steps through it.

"Frannie," Samantha said after a long time had gone by. We were at the creek now. From here, Samantha would go right down Eastbay Road to her house, and I would continue on North Conduit, walking with the highway to the left of me to my apartment building. There were some dark clouds over our heads.

"What if that boy really *is* Jesus? What if Jesus did come here, to where we live?"

"Jesus who?"

"Jesus-Jesus, that's who. God's son. Think about it, Frannie. In the Bible, he just showed up and then miracles started happening—people started rising up from the dead and eating bread that was his body and drinking wine that was his blood and—"

"Yuck!" I said, covering my ears. "Yuck on the blood-wine. Yuck on the body-bread. Yuck on the dead walking back into the world after we went and had a whole expensive funeral for them."

Samantha stared at me. "Listen to me," she said, trying to sound like a very patient grown-up. "If there was a world for Jesus to need to walk back into, wouldn't this one be it?"

We stopped walking.

"There's a war going on—"

"Yeah," I said, "and it's been going on since the sixties and before that there was one in the forties and the twenties and the tens—there's always a war going on somewhere—how come Jesus didn't choose one of those? Or how come he didn't come back and stop this one all those years ago when it started. And plus—Jesus wasn't a *boy*."

"People starving," Samantha said, ignoring me and counting off her fingers.

"Dust bowl. Depression," I said, counting off my own.

"Hurricanes, tornadoes."

"Dorothy. Toto."

Samantha rolled her eyes at me and started walking again. "You think I'm kidding around. And when did you start listening in social studies anyway?"

"It sinks in when I sleep, I guess."

I didn't say anything else, just started walking beside her.

Samantha's father preached at his own church, OnePeople Baptist, over near the mall. Mama called it a fire-and-brimstone church because either you were holy or you weren't. Either you were gonna burn in eternal fire or go to

33

heaven. There wasn't some in-between. *I'm neither holy enough nor bad enough to go to his church,* Mama had said. But every Sunday, Samantha was there, sitting right up front with her mother, listening to every single word.

Most Sundays, I could find a hundred excuses not to go to church with my parents. Even Sean got up to go more than me.

My grandmother went to *two* churches on Sunday. In the morning she went to church with my parents. And in the afternoon she went to a different church—one she'd been going to forever. During the week, she read her Bible, so it was always in her bag and sometimes she took it out and tapped me on the head with it, saying, *Maybe the information in here will get into your head that way.* And if I decided I wanted to say something dumb in front of her—like *Jesus Christ!* after I stubbed my toe or something—then the tap wasn't so soft. Wasn't soft at all. As a matter of fact, my grandmother could knock you good on your head with her Bible if she wanted to. Once I'd even said, *I don't think God meant for his good book to be a weapon, Grandma.* She chucked me a good one and said, *Isn't no weapon—just what I have handy, that's all.*

Even with all the churchgoing happening around me, I'd never thought of Jesus as being much of anything. I mean, if people needed to believe he was God's son and he walked the earth and blah, blah, blah, I wasn't going to tell them they were wrong or right about their ideas about things. I was just going to do like I did with my grandmother—nod and hold my tongue and duck if the Bible came flying.

Samantha lifted her book bag onto her shoulder. "I mean, it's all so strange, don't you think? He came to our school in the middle of the year. And it's like he came from *nowhere*." She looked at me.

"He came from across the highway, Samantha. He said so."

"It's still strange—the way he just showed up. Who crosses the highway to come *here* to live? Nobody. It had to be for some *reason*."

"He said his family didn't belong there."

"Jesus wandered the earth that same way—looking for a place where he could be accepted. How surreal is that?"

I tried to find the word *surreal* in my mental vocabulary bank where Ms. Johnson had said we should save vocabulary words so that we could grow up and have rich brains, but it wasn't there. Ms. Johnson said the only way you can deposit a word in your bank is by committing it to memory. I hadn't deposited *surreal*. I guess I must have spent it somewhere.

"Yeah, it is surreal, I guess," I said. "Real surreal."

"You know what the shortest verse in the Bible is?" Samantha said. Her Bible bank was probably as rich as her vocabulary bank.

"Well, *do* you?" Samantha asked again.

I shrugged. "You know I'm not churchgoing, Sam. I can't even remember half my *schoolwork* most days, how'm I gonna know what's in the Bible? All I know is it's just the right size for Grandma to smack against my head every time she gets a need to, that's for sure." I laughed, but Samantha didn't. Samantha was on my side about the Bible thing. She'd even

35

said to Grandma once—"That's not the Lord's purpose for that book, Ms. Wright." But my grandmother just said, "Thank you, Miss Samantha."

"It goes 'Jesus wept,' " Samantha said. "Isn't that strange?"

I shrugged. "People cry sometimes. Even teachers and moms and stuff. Even you and me," I said.

Samantha looked at me. "Yeah—but if Abigail Francesca Wright Barnes cried, it wouldn't get put into a book that millions of billions of people would read."

"Maybe it would. If I did it in front of the right person at the right time. I could be inspiring. Maybe not a whole lot of people know me now, but—"

"It's just all so surreal," Samantha said again. "You wake up one day and it's wintertime and there's snow falling. You wake another day and there's a new boy in your class with wild hair, named Jesus."

"That's not his real name, though."

"Jesus wept," she said again. "Isn't that strange?" She put her hands in her coat pockets. The coat was pink with a white fur collar and hood. I remembered it from last year, when the sleeves were rolled up. Now the coat fit perfectly and Samantha looked real pretty inside of it. She'd gotten taller than me and I had to look up just a little bit when I talked to her.

"He's just some boy, Samantha. Nothing strange about that at all. And plus—Jesus wasn't white—even your daddy says so. White people drew all those white-person pictures of Jesus, but that wasn't his real color. You know that. That Jesus Boy is white."

The wind was blowing hard—a high whistling sound.

"He said he's not white," Samantha said.

"That boy is white, Samantha! You could almost see through his skin. He's like blue-white! That's even whiter than white."

"But," Samantha said calmly, "he says he's not white. We don't know what the world looks like from inside his eyes. For all we know, *you're* white."

"What?!"

Samantha looked confused, like she was just realizing what she was saying. After a moment, her face changed, though, and she smiled.

"Maybe Jesus is the color he needs to be when he comes to a place, Frannie. Maybe this time around he needs to be a skinny white boy—something way different from everything around him."

I shrugged. "As long as you're not trying to make the brother-man brown, girl."

"I don't think I'll mention it to Daddy, though," Samantha said, looking at me.

"Well, you know *I'm* not saying anything about it. It would be up there with me saying you believed in the Tooth Fairy and Santa, wouldn't it?"

Samantha smiled and shook her head. She started walking backwards away from me, waving good-bye to me as she walked. Then she turned and walked faster. I watched her head down Eastbay Road, getting smaller and smaller. I stood there a long time, shivering in the cold. A part of me stood there promising myself that from now on, I'd go to church more and listen to my grandma when she started preaching.

But another part of me knew that the part of myself that was making those promises was lying. The wind got harder and I hugged myself. I stood there wishing I knew what the word *surreal* meant—I knew I wouldn't go home and look it up— I'm just not that kinda person. But standing there in the cold and the wind, the word felt big and important to me—like it was trying to wrap itself around me—like it was tapping itself on my head, trying to get in.

I touched the frozen creek with the toe of my boot. Tiny spider lines spread everywhere. I squatted down and stared at them. My face looked long and brown and shadowy in the reflection. It looked like it was breaking into a million pieces. Some mornings, I woke up feeling like the whole world was slipping away from me. Mama said it was just growing pains and soon they'd go away. I got up and turned around, wanting to yell for Samantha, wanting to hear her say some more about . . . about anything. She had all kinds of things she could believe in. Big and surreal things that took up her mind and got her thinking deep and smiling that secret I-know-some-things smile.

I stood there watching her walk away. It wasn't that she *did* believe that the Jesus Boy was really Jesus—it was that she *could*. I couldn't. No way. It was too crazy, too way out there. Too . . . too far away for me. The snow was starting to come down hard again. And in the distance, the only thing I could see was little specks of Samantha's bright pink coat—far away from me, fading in and out. In and out.

PART THREE

7

"Mama," I called, taking my boots off and leaving my knapsack by the door.

Sean came out of Mama's room, frowning and waving his hand.

She's sleeping, he signed, his hand moving over his face like it was pulling his eyes closed.

It's not even four o'clock, I signed back, saying the words at the same time. Sean could read lips, but most times I was thinking too fast to talk slow enough for him to understand me, so I just signed right back at him.

She's tired, Frannie.

I felt something jump inside of me. Something hard and heavy.

Don't start your stupid worrying, Sean said. *She's just feeling tired.*

Three years ago, Mama started complaining about her belly hurting. It took a long time for everybody to convince her to go to the doctor. She was still shaken from losing Baby Lila and the miscarriage she'd had a year after that, so hospitals and doctors made her nervous.

"They always find something wrong," she said, drinking mint tea to calm the pain. But the pain didn't get calm and a few weeks later, she went to the Emergency Room. That night, we found out that she'd had a baby growing but the baby wasn't *thriving*. That's the word the doctor used. *Thriving*. And the next year, when my fourth-grade teacher said to Mama, *Frannie isn't thriving in science and math*, my mama's face had clouded over and tears came to her eyes.

Mama stayed in the hospital for a long time after the not-thriving baby died. And the whole time she was in there, it felt like our family was holding its breath. Then, when the doctors said she was okay, we all started breathing again. But Mama came home quiet and sad and for a long time that's how she stayed.

But the weeks passed and Mama got better. Every morning, she'd get out of bed and hug me and Sean, calling us her gifts from God, her unbroken promises, her little lives. And some mornings, I'd find her sitting holding the framed picture of Lila she kept at her bedside, a sadness on her face so deep, it seemed like no one would ever be able to break through it.

The years passed and the sadness went away too. Mama laughed more and hugged us all the time. She and Daddy headed back to their church, and slowly, our house became this new kind of normal.

She's supposed to be all better, I signed, slinking down against the wall. I felt like I was eight years old again, scared and mad at Mama for not being Mama. She had *said* she was all better.

Sean smiled and shook his head. It wasn't a big smile. Just more like a big-brother smile. He's so beautiful—all tall and dark with pretty eyes and a nice big-brother smile. If he wasn't deaf, he'd have a million girlfriends. Hearing girls were always looking at him. But most times, when they saw his hands flying through the air, they stopped looking, which was stupid to me. Sign language is just another language and if they weren't so dumb, maybe they could learn to speak it. Once in a while, he'd tell us about a deaf girl in his school that liked him. Sometimes he liked her back. Sometimes he didn't.

She IS all better, Sean signed. *Just relax. Help me make some dinner.*

I don't want to make any dinner, I signed. *I want to kiss Mama's head.*

Then go kiss it already!

I tiptoed down the hall and stopped to look at the picture of Lila. Her dark eyes stared back at me. Sometimes, Mama talked about the Baby Heaven—where Lila and the two other babies had gone—how maybe there was a whole other Wright-Barnes family up there, fussing and laughing, eating and singing. I stood there staring at the picture. If Jesus came back to this world—I don't know what I'd want from him. I know what I'd ask, though. I'd say, "Mr. Jesus, I'm sorry to bother you but I have a question. I wanted to know how do you have hope?" I'd want to know how do you have hope when there's always a Trevor somewhere kicking at somebody. When there's always a mama somewhere who maybe wasn't *thriving.* And maybe he would look at me and smile the way Sean smiled—all patient and sorry for me. Maybe he'd have that calm look like the Jesus Boy.

Maybe he'd have an answer.

I opened Mama's door slowly and kneeled down beside her bed. It was almost dark now and the light coming into her room was silvery and soft. Everything was so quiet, I could hear my own breath and hers too, coming slowly. Her mouth was slightly open and she looked real peaceful with her eyes closed and that little bit of silver light coming in on her dark face. She had the most perfect nose—not too big and not too small. I ran my finger over her eyebrows. They were thick and then they got thin at the edges because she tweezes them that way. One day I'd get my eyebrows tweezed—even if it hurt—just so they could be perfect like Mama's. And maybe I'd get some false eyelashes so mine could be long and dark and beautiful like hers. I sat on her bed, pushed her hair away from her forehead and kissed it. Mama opened her eyes.

"Stop worrying," she whispered. "I see you setting your mind to worrying already. I'm just tired, that's all." Mama looked like she wanted to say something more but then didn't.

She closed her eyes again. After a few minutes had passed, she opened them, looked at me and smiled.

"Frannie. Everything's gonna be fine. *I'm* fine."

"Then why are you sleeping in the daytime?" I moved a little bit closer to her. Her body felt warm.

"Because your mama gets tired sometimes—dealing with all you kids."

"It's just . . . just me and Sean. We're not *that* much work."

"Already feels like more most days."

"What do you mean—it already feels like more?"

Mama touched me on the cheek. "I don't want you worrying, Frannie. That's all I'm saying, okay?"

I nodded.

"Wait until you have two, then you can come talk to me about what's a lot and what's not a lot." Mama smiled. I tried to move closer.

"Why don't you just sit on top of me, girl?" she said, moving over on the bed.

"I want you to get up now," I said. I knew I sounded whiny but I didn't care.

Mama sighed. "I can't, Frannie. Not right now. In a little while, okay? I promise you."

She looked at me. My face must have been all worried-looking because she said, "What's that old Maribel Tanks talking about these days?"

"Samantha sat down right at her table! And then I had to sit there because Samantha was sitting there and then Maribel was talking about stinky pennies that the Jesus Boy—"

Mama closed her eyes. "The who . . . ," she said softly.

"The new boy. Everybody is saying he looks like Jesus, only I don't think so because he's just a kid and all—just that his hair is all—"

I could hear Mama breathing slowly. Maybe she was already asleep.

"Mama?"

"Yes, baby."

"What's . . . what's *surreal*?"

"Your voice going when I'm almost asleep."

"No it isn't. I mean, is that what it *means*?"

"Like a dream," Mama said softly. "Like something not feeling like it could be really happening. Does that make sense, sweetie?"

I nodded. "Yeah. Like that boy just showing up . . . like he was showing up in somebody's dream. And then you wake up and maybe he's not there anymore."

"Or maybe he is but it's not as strange. People always wonder about the new kid—you know that. You were the new kid once."

"Only by a month and that was because of the stupid chicken pox!"

"But everyone looked at you like you were from the moon. At least that's how you described it."

I tried to move closer to Mama some more. "Well, they *did* stare."

"Of course they did, boo," Mama said. "We told you again and again not to scratch and you scratched anyway, so you had scabs all over your body. I would stare too. Thank God for vitamin E."

"It didn't clear them all up," I said, holding out my arm. "I still have the two pockmarks on my hands and some—"

"On your leg. I know, baby. Maybe *your* daughter will listen when you tell her not to scratch! Go help Sean get dinner going. I'm just going to rest a few minutes, then I'll get on up."

I kissed her forehead but didn't move.

"Your mama sure is tired this evening . . ." She didn't finish. After a while, her breath started coming all even and I knew she was asleep.

"It's all so surreal," I whispered, stroking her forehead. Outside, the sky was getting darker. "Some days, it feels like it's always gonna be wintertime."

Mama reached up and pressed her hand on top of mine. We stayed like that for a long time.

8

Sean could do three things real well—he could play basketball, he could do math, and he could season chicken. Once he tried to show me how to do the chicken, but mine came out tasting salty and bitter.

You gonna help or what? Sean said. He was chopping up carrots and onions.

I said I would, right?

Well, don't touch any spices, he said, pointing to the spice shelf, giving me a look. *Especially the salt. You can put these in those bowls. I'm going to cook them with the broccoli.*

I put the carrots and onions in the bowls he'd put on the table. *Broccoli's only good with cheese.*

He opened the refrigerator and stood there smelling different packages, trying to figure out what to cook and what had gone bad. *You'd put cheese on everything if you could.* He threw a package into the garbage can and took out some chopped meat. *Burgers and vegetables.*

And rice, I said. *I can make rice. It's easy.*

Sean looked at me. *When you make it, it's like oatmeal. Rice should be all separate. Yours is all sticky.*

No it's not! You're just mad because I make it better than you!

You're dreaming, Sean said. But he reached up in the cabinet and handed me the box of rice. *Don't put a whole lot of salt in it. And make sure you put a little butter in the water.*

I didn't say anything. He knew I was the better rice maker.

Sean started shaping the meat into patties. He took a pan out of the oven and put a little oil in it.

You think Mama's gonna be okay, Sean? I asked after a few minutes had passed.

He nodded and watched me put the rice and water in a pot.

Two cups of water, he said.

One and a half. That's how Mama does it. I put a little more than Mama but less than what Sean was saying. Then I put some salt and a little bit of butter in the pot and waited for it to boil.

Sean reached over me and stirred it. *If you don't stir it before it starts boiling, it sticks.*

Yours sticks! My rice is always perfect!

I heard the front door close.

Daddy's home! I signed, leaving Sean standing there stirring my rice.

Daddy stood in the long hall leading into our apartment, grinning and holding flowers. Everyone said I was going to be tall like him one day, but it wasn't the tallness I wanted. I wanted his laugh—all loud and silly. And his smile that came into the room a full minute before he did. And I wanted his pretty eyes—the ones Sean got—and his dark, pretty skin that Mama swore I had, but my skin always looked to me like it didn't know what shade it wanted to be—dark in some places, lighter in other spots.

49

Daddy stepped out of his shoes and took his wet coat off at the same time. I ran down the hall and jumped into his arms, my legs dangling almost to the floor, Sean right behind me.

Daddy laughed, walking into the apartment with both of us hanging on to him.

"I guess I need to go away more often," he said, signing at the same time. Sean grinned and shook his head. Daddy drove a truck for Interstate Moving and had been away since Wednesday—moving some family's stuff to Indiana. Now it was Friday. His goneness felt like forever sometimes.

You need a job that doesn't make you go away, Sean signed.

"Where's my *woman*?!" Daddy said, loud. He shook us off of him and did his caveman walk into the living room. "I'm hungry and I'm tired! And why can't this man smell something good cooking?"

"Mama's resting," I said.

Sean looked at me. He signed, *I'm cooking. Mama's not feeling well,* and Daddy's smile dropped off his face. He dumped the flowers onto the coffee table and headed to Mama's room.

I picked up the flowers—they were pretty—yellow and red and white with green leaves bunched around them.

Hey, big brother, what kind are these. I held the flowers toward him.

Lily. He finger-spelled the word for me. *And roses. The red and white ones are roses. You know that!* he signed. *Must be payday. Flowers cost a lot in the wintertime.*

When I have a daughter, I signed, *her name will be LilyRose.*

Sean made a face and headed back into the kitchen. I followed him.

Your rice is boiling.

I turned the fire down underneath the pot and covered it.

Sean got the jar that Mama used for flowers down from the shelf. I filled it with water and put the flowers in slowly. Sean pulled down plates and took forks out of the drawer. He put four glasses on the kitchen table—we didn't have a dining room but our kitchen was big enough for four people to move around in.

Then, without saying anything, he put the burgers on, washed his hands, put some oil in another pan and started cooking the carrots.

What about the onions and broccoli, I said. *And cheese?*

Sean took a deep breath. *Carrots take the longest. So you have to cook them first. Then onions. Then broccoli. Then a tiny bit of salt. Not a whole lot like you think everything needs.* He stirred the carrots, then covered them. The only sound was the sound of things frying.

Sean watched me take a red rose and move it closer to a white one, then I thought for a moment and put a lily and some of the green leaves between the two.

He turned back to the stove, flipped the burgers, then tore a paper bag in half and put a big piece of it on a plate. Then he added the onions to the carrots, stirred and covered the pan again. He went back over to the refrigerator and opened it. Then just stood there, staring inside. He had ears like Mama, small and perfect shaped. When he was born, the doctors had wanted to do some new kind of operation to fix the inside of them, but Mama and Daddy said no.

Nobody's experimenting on my child, Mama said. *If that's the way he came into the world, that's the way he's staying. It's us we need to change.* And she and Daddy started learning sign language. By the time I was born, Sean was two and a half years old. I grew up learning how to speak and sign. Sometimes, when he walked past her, Mama just grabbed him and kissed his ears. Sean always laughed but he pushed her away at the same time. I wondered if he was standing staring into the refrigerator thinking about that.

Years later, when I asked Mama why they didn't just get the operation, she said because it was dangerous and not guaranteed. *And most of all,* she said, signing at the same time, *there's nothing wrong about being deaf. It's just another language. So now you're bilingual,* Mama said. *That's a gift.*

That was the first and last time anybody said anything about *me* being gifted.

I waved my hand at Sean to get his attention. He liked that more than somebody coming up and touching him.

The ocean, I signed.

Sean shrugged.

Water, he signed, *water and air. It sounds the way air feels on your face on a windy day.*

He took some ketchup out of the refrigerator and one slice of cheese.

Here, he signed, putting the cheese down on one of the plates. *That's where you sit.*

Yellow, he signed.

That's a hard one, Sean! Yellow doesn't have a SOUND.

Nothing has a sound to me! That's how this game got started. Yellow!

52

We'd been playing this game since we were real little. One person gave the word and the other person had to describe it, to make the person feel it someplace inside of themselves. To make the person *hear* it. Sean was better at the game than me, but I still loved playing.

Like something soft, I signed. *A pillow.* Or yellow *sounds like bubbles feel—lots of them in a bathtub.*

Sean nodded. Then he turned the fire off beneath the burgers and put each of them on the plate with the paper bag. I watched the bag get dark from the oil.

He stirred the onions again, added some spices, a little bit of butter and the broccoli, then stirred it once more, added some water, turned the heat down beneath it and covered the pan.

Music, I said.

What kind? He looked at my rice, then raised his eyebrows.

I turned it off but didn't lift the top. *Perfect,* I said. *A guitar.*

Sean thought for a minute. *Like rain,* he said. *Coming down real soft when it's warm out and you only get a little wet but not cold. That kind of rain.*

I smiled. That's exactly what it made me feel like when I heard a guitar playing softly.

Daddy came out of the bedroom. We watched his face. His eyebrow twitched. You had to look hard to see it.

Let her rest a bit, he said finally. *Dinner ready? Smells good in here.*

For a while, we ate without doing much talking. I watched the cheese melt on my burger, then poured ketchup over everything, stirred my rice until it turned pink. We listened for Mama to come out of her room but she didn't.

"Anything interesting happen at school this week?" Daddy asked. He took a bite of his vegetables and smiled at Sean. Me and Sean both shook our heads.

"Nothing interesting happened with work either," Daddy said softly. "The road from here to Indiana is flat as my feet. Every now and then a bright green road sign pops up to keep you awake."

"Is Indiana pretty?" I asked.

Daddy thought for a minute. "Pretty light when the sun's coming up. But what place ain't pretty at the beginning and the end of the day?"

Where's the prettiest place you ever been, Daddy?

Daddy grinned. "I guess California. Took me a long time to drive there, but when I got there, I went straight to the ocean. It was almost night when I pulled the truck up to where I could see the water." He closed his eyes a moment. "All those different colors spilling over everything." Then he opened his eyes and looked at me and Sean. "And here," he said.

Sean watched his lips. When Daddy finished speaking, Sean kept on watching them. After a while, Daddy got up from the table, scraped the food off his plate and put the plate in the sink.

I watched Sean watch Daddy. Sometimes he just stared— and it was like his eyes were trying to do everything—speak and hear and smell and touch. Maybe that's why they were so beautiful. They had all the senses right there in them, showing through.

There's another one coming, Daddy signed. *Another baby.* He smiled—a kind of laugh smile like he was just as surprised as we were by what he was hearing.

What?!

Another baby, Daddy said again.

That's crazy! Mama's too old. We're all too old. What's anybody in this house gonna do with a baby?

Sean smiled, like it was all slowly sinking in and he liked what was becoming clear or something. *A baby,* he signed. *Wow.* He leaned back in his chair and stared out the kitchen window. Snow was still coming down hard. *A baby,* he signed again.

I ran my fork through my rice, feeling all kinds of stupid feelings. *I* was the baby who *had* made it. It was sad, but each time one of those other babies didn't make it, it seemed clear to me that I was the one who was *supposed* to be the baby in the family.

"I don't know why she has to be so tired about it all," I said. "Doesn't make any sense." I didn't say what I really wanted to say. *What if you and Mama come home crying again,* I wanted to ask. *What if we think a baby's coming but it doesn't come all the way?*

Daddy looked at me. "Because you're right, Frannie. She *is* old. And that makes it harder to be pregnant. And . . ." But he shook his head and didn't finish what he was going to say. After a minute passed, he signed, *So let her get some rest and try to grow you all a brother or sister.*

I shrugged. "Even if it's a girl, I'm not sharing my room, that's for sure."

Daddy ignored me. *Sean, you wash tonight,* he signed. *Frannie, you dry and wipe everything down.*

I don't want to wash! Sean glared at Daddy. *I always have to wash.*

Because you always get them clean, Daddy said. *Frannie, you wash the dishes then!*

I shrugged. I didn't mind washing—the warm water felt good in the wintertime. And the bubbles were fun to squeeze through my hands.

Forget it, Sean signed. *She doesn't know how to do it. We'll be eating hamburgers and rice off our plates for a week. I'll wash.*

Daddy put his hands up. "Ain't that where we started?" he said. *Come say good night to your mama before you go to bed, you hear.*

Me and Sean nodded. Then Sean got up and started in on the dishes. Somewhere, in another apartment, somebody was playing music—the same song over and over again. It never felt right, to be hearing the song and not have Sean hearing it too. I knew he had his own music going inside his head, music I'd never be able to hear, and maybe that made *him* sad. But still, sometimes when I heard music, even if Sean was right next to me, I missed him. I got up and took my plate over to the sink. Me and Sean didn't even look at each other but I bumped him with my shoulder on purpose and he bumped me right back. For some strange reason, it was enough for both of us, just to be standing side by side.

9

Mama stayed in bed on Saturday, only getting up to go to the bathroom and to stop me from yelling at Sean for changing the television channel in the middle of my favorite cartoons. It was almost noon when she came into the living room. There were bags under her eyes and when she signed to Sean, her hands moved slower than usual. Sean was in a stupid mood and needed to be fighting with somebody.

She's been watching it all morning, he said.

"I just watched—"

Mama put her hand up. *You two need to figure it out . . .*

"Forget it. Let him watch whatever he wants. I don't care. I gotta clean the stupid bathroom anyway." I was talking with my back to Sean so that he couldn't see my lips. He hated when I did that but I didn't care. I stomped down the hall and started pulling the cleaning supplies out of the hallway closet. I hated seeing Mama looking all tired and messy. It wasn't fair. Let Sean watch whatever he wanted, it didn't matter to me. I just wanted her to go back to bed and come out of her room looking better. Sean was so stupid sometimes. He acted like he didn't even care.

After a little while, I heard him flick the television off, head to his room and slam the door.

The apartment got quiet and the quiet felt like something hot and sticky all over me. Something scary and all blurred up. I leaned over the edge of the tub to scrub it. Snow had piled up outside the bathroom window and the sky was silvery-gray—like something heavy was pushing down on the clouds. For some reason the Jesus Boy came into my mind. I wondered where he lived, what he was doing. I wondered if he had a window to stare out of and watch snow coming down. When I tried to picture his face, all I saw was the broken-up look he'd had that afternoon. I tried to think about the real Jesus, the one Samantha knew so well. All I kept seeing was hands, though—hands and feet with scars on them.

While I was scrubbing, the sun came out—watery and cold-looking. I sat on the edge of the tub with my sponge in one hand and the can of Comet in the other. Just sat there like that, watching the sky until the sun faded back behind the clouds again.

After I finished cleaning the bathroom, me and Daddy went grocery shopping. We got onto the elevator and Daddy took my hand. I knew I was too big for that but I let him take it anyway. When the elevator started moving again, I took a deep breath and let it out slowly.

"What's going on, star?" he asked. His voice sounded strange in the closed elevator. Sometimes I forgot how quiet it was inside our house with all that signing going on and all.

I shrugged.

"You worrying, aren't you?"

"Aren't *you*?" I looked up at him. His eyes were red and

puffy and he hadn't shaved. "Those other babies . . . ," I said slowly. "They . . . they *died*. Mama grew them for a while and then they were all gone again."

Daddy pulled me closer to him. "Here's the deal," he said. The elevator door opened and we walked out into the lobby past the weekend doorman. The lobby had mirrors and pretty tile floors and a fake fireplace with an electric log in it.

"You don't need to worry about what happened before. All you need to look at is what's happening now." He nudged my chin up so I would look at him. "And be happy about it. And if it means you only get to be happy for a month or two months or three months, so what. A month or two months or three months is a good long time."

I kept looking up at him. My head felt like it was all swirly inside. Felt like if somebody lifted the ground out from beneath me, I'd just float off somewhere. I shivered, took my hand out of Daddy's and shoved it in my pocket.

When I was a little girl, Sean would stand over me and sign songs. When my brother danced, it was like nothing else mattered anywhere. He danced and signed like there was music all around him all the time. Some days, I wished I could hear that music. And some days I wished I could climb inside all the quiet and stillness inside Sean's head, curl up there and just rest awhile.

Daddy opened the car door and I climbed into the back. He always promised me I would be able to sit up front next year. Every year was next year.

He got in on the driver's side and started the car. It was an old car and needed a few minutes to warm up.

"This tiredness could just be," Daddy said, "that your mama's been working too hard and you kids—"

"Been wearing her out," I finished for him, rolling my eyes. With all the wearing out of my mama she and Daddy said we did, you'd think she'd be completely see-through by now. Like the old pieces of cotton sheets we used to dust with. I stared out the window.

My grandmother always says that good things come in ones and twos and threes and bad things come however they can get here. I tried to close my eyes and picture the place where all the tiredness was coming from, the place where the baby was growing and wearing Mama out. I wanted to lift the tiredness up out of Mama with my thinking. I wanted powers like that. If I could walk through the world and just touch people and lift their pains right out of their bodies, I'd never stop walking. I looked down at the pocks on my palms. They were starting to itch.

"What you thinking about, sweet pea," Daddy asked.

"Nothing," I said.

I kept staring out the window, silently scratching my palms.

10

I asked Daddy to drop me off at the rec center after we finished grocery shopping. I wanted to watch Sean playing ball.

"You going there to play some games or you going there to bother your brother?" Daddy asked, pulling up in front of the gray building kids went to after school sometimes and on weekends. The building always smelled sweaty and the sound of kids running around the gym and game room echoed all over the place, then got all muffled—like the noises were drowning in their own sound.

"He won't care," I said. Once he got used to the idea that he'd have to walk home with me, I figured, he'd just have to accept it. It's not like I followed him around *that* much.

Daddy rolled his window down and I leaned in and kissed him on the cheek.

"You two be careful," he said, rolling up the window real fast so the snow wouldn't blow in.

I shivered, pulled my hat down over my ears, and ran inside.

The minute Sean saw me, he frowned. Two of the guys he was playing with were deaf and one of them signed, *Babysitting time.*

Sean signed a curse back. One that a lot of hearing people knew.

He chucked the ball to another guy and took a time-out, coming over to me. He was wearing a pair of old blue shorts and a T-shirt that had this cartoon guy walking down the street in a long robe. Underneath the guy, it said KEEP ON TRUCKING. The shirt used to belong to Daddy but somehow Sean had inherited it. There was a big dark patch of sweat under his collar.

What are you doing here? he asked.

I shrugged. *There wasn't anything to do at home.*

Sean looked at me. One of the guys was waving for him to come on and Sean signed for him to wait.

Can't you see he's talking, I said, and Sean gave me a look.

Sit down, he said. *I'm almost done.* He tapped me on the head and ran back over to his game.

The tap on the head meant he wasn't mad at me for coming. I climbed onto the bleachers and sat down in front of some girls who were watching the game.

"That's your brother?" one of them asked me.

I looked at her and nodded, then turned back front.

"He can't hear *anything*?" I heard her asking my back.

I knew what was coming, so I didn't turn around again. "Nope."

"Dag," she said. "That's messed up."

I heard another girl say, "And he's a fine brother-man too."

I rolled my eyes and felt my hands clinching inside my coat pockets.

"No wonder he's not trying to talk to us."

I wanted to say, "He's not trying to talk to you because he's not interested in you!" But I didn't say anything. What was the use? Instead, I watched Sean and his friends play full court. Sean took a shot and missed, then looked over at me and shrugged. Then he looked at the girls behind me and ducked his head a bit before taking off down the court.

"Those other two guys are deaf too," another one of the girls said.

"Yeah—but they're not as cute as her brother."

There were three hearing guys playing against Sean and his friends. From the looks of it, the hearing guys were winning. I didn't want to see that. Not with those dumb girls behind me. Not with the deaf guys trying so hard and all. I got up after a few more minutes and signed to Sean that I'd meet him in the hallway. He nodded and I left the gym. Kids were running around and there were a few grown-ups trying to get them to use "walking feet."

I leaned against the wall, watching it all. There was a poster across from me listing all the rules of the rec center. Next to each rule, instead of a number, there was a big yellow smiley face. Next to the rule that said NO GRAFFITI, somebody had Magic-Markered their name and a frowning face.

I was smiling over that when I saw the Jesus Boy coming out of the boys' locker room, zipping up his coat, his hair wet and curling over his shoulders. I stopped smiling. Maybe he felt me staring because he looked up suddenly.

I just kept staring at him.

"Hey," he said when he got a little bit closer.

"Hey yourself."

"What're you doing here, Frannie?"

It felt strange to hear him say my name.

"It's a free country."

He moved a little bit closer to me. "That's what they say." He signed the word *say*.

"How come you know sign anyway?"

The Jesus Boy stopped smiling, thought for a minute, then shrugged. "I don't know," he said slowly, like he was really trying to understand.

"That doesn't make any sense."

"I just know it," he said. "I just do. Maybe from when I was a baby or something."

"Well, it's not something a person's born knowing," I said.

"Well, how come you know English?"

"Because my family knows English and that's what they taught me."

Jesus Boy shrugged again. "So maybe it's the same for me. Maybe somebody in my family knew it one time."

I shook my head. "That doesn't make even a little bit of sense."

"Does to me," he said.

"Do they sign now?"

He made the sign for *maybe* and smiled at me.

I signed back, *Maybe you're crazy.*

"Well, what made you sign to *me* the other day?" I asked.

"I saw you walking with that guy who signs. You two were talking to each other."

"That's my brother," I said. "Sean."

"Yeah," Jesus Boy said. "I was kinda far away when I saw you, but y'all look alike."

"No we don't," I said. Sean was beautiful. Everybody could see that. I was just regular.

We just sort of stood there for a while, watching people go by.

"I'm waiting for my dad," Jesus Boy said. "Maybe I should be waiting outside."

"Well, good-bye then," I said.

The Jesus Boy looked at me sideways but didn't move.

"You really lived across the highway?" I asked.

Jesus Boy nodded.

"What was *that* like? To live over there."

"It would have been okay for me. But it wasn't okay for my mom and dad," he said. "It was hard for them. People can be so stupid. Once this cop stopped us and asked me if I knew my dad. Me and my dad were fooling around, kinda wrestling and stuff. He thought my dad was hurting me."

He looked at me, then said, "I don't look like him, I guess."

"How come."

He stared at the poster with the smiley faces. "Just 'cause. It doesn't really matter. I used to wish that I would wake up and look just like him. I still do sometimes. I look at him and he's so cool and . . ." He stopped.

I watched him, waiting for him to say something more, but he didn't. Just put his hands in his pockets and stood there.

Two little kids ran by us but slowed down to stare at him. At us.

"Take a picture," I said. "It lasts longer." The little girl stuck her tongue out at me, then she and her friend ran off.

Jesus Boy smiled. His eyeteeth were kind of fangy.

Someone pulled the rec center door open and a group of boys came in making a lot of noise. I could see Trevor in the middle of them, his coat hanging off the arm that had the cast on it. When he saw us, he stopped.

"If it ain't Mr. and Mrs. Jesus," he said. The other guys with him looked at us. One of them laughed.

"You still here?"

The Jesus Boy looked at him. "I'm still here."

One of the guys said "C'mon, Trev" as they started walking away. Trevor told them to go ahead, he'd catch up.

"You know I don't even like you," Trevor said.

"You don't even know me, man."

"I ain't your man, white boy!"

The Jesus Boy looked at him calmly and said, "Well, I ain't your white boy, man."

"We could take this outside," Trevor said.

"You go ahead," the Jesus Boy said. "I'll meet you there."

Trevor looked at him, his blue eyes getting smaller and more evil.

I wanted to ask him what he planned to do with his arm in a cast and all but then the door opened and a tall, dark-skinned man came in, looked around, then saw us.

"You ready," he said to the Jesus Boy.

The Jesus Boy nodded. "This is Frannie. Frannie, this is my pops. That's Trevor."

I felt my eyebrows lifting up and tried to make them go down again.

"Hey Frannie."

I managed to say hello but Trevor just stood there a moment, staring at the man. Then, without saying anything, he turned and took off down the hall.

The little girls were back, staring at all three of us now.

"Let's get moving," Jesus Boy's dad said. "We got things to do."

As they were leaving, I heard him ask the Jesus Boy how his swim was. I couldn't hear the answer.

"Is that white boy your boyfriend?" one of the little girls asked.

I had forgotten they were standing there.

"Oh, scat out of here already," I said, waving my hands at them. They squealed and ran off again.

But later on, when Sean came out of the gym all sweaty and pulling on his coat, I was still thinking about the Jesus Boy and his daddy.

You're always following me, Sean signed.

You like it, I signed back.

How come you didn't watch the whole game? We went crazy on those guys. They didn't know what was happening to them once we got warmed up! You missed my winning shot. He took a jump shot, throwing his basketball into the air and catching it.

I thought about the stupid girls in the bleachers, then brushed the thought out of my head.

It got too hot in there, I signed. *And stinky.*

Sean laughed and chucked me on the head again.

Down the hall, I could see Trevor and his friends standing around in a circle. I heard the guard telling them to get out of the hallway and saw Trevor give the guard a mean look.

"You can get out of my hallway or you can leave," the guard said.

"Let's go play some pinball," one of the boys said, and the others followed him down the hall to the game room. "C'mon, lefty," he said, looking at Trevor. "Let's see what you got with that one good hand." Trevor smiled and his face looked almost normal—soft and happy.

Isn't that kid in your class? Sean asked.

I nodded.

How come you didn't go hang with him then?

I watched Trevor move down the hall with his friends. *I don't like him.*

Beggars can't be choosy, Sean said, smiling and tapping my head again.

I know, I said. *That's why I'm stuck with you!*

And as we walked out into the snow, I lifted my head up to catch flakes on my tongue, feeling them melting in my mouth and, somehow, warming me.

11

Late in the afternoon, I was sitting with Sean on the couch, eating pretzels and cheese. We weren't allowed to eat sugar when the weather was real bad because Mama said it made us too crazy with all the running around and jumping up and down we did. But Sean had picked up a Hershey bar on the way home and we'd split it and stuffed it into our mouths before we got on the elevator. I felt like I'd bounce off the ceiling and ricochet all over the apartment if the snow didn't stop.

The weather guy had said this was a record—that it hadn't snowed this much since way back in the fifties. I'd turned on the radio and the Jackson 5 were singing "ABC." I was in love with Michael Jackson. He was one of the cutest boys on the planet as far as I knew. I got off the couch and started dancing to the song. Mama had gotten me a rainbow peasant skirt for Christmas and when I twirled in it, the colors seemed to spread light all over the room. Sean shook his head watching me. He signed, *One of these days, I'm gonna teach you some rhythm.* When the music was loud enough, Sean could feel the rhythm through the vibration. When he danced, you wouldn't even know he was deaf. But he was too busy stuffing pretzels in his mouth and making fun of me to get up off the couch and move around.

The music was so loud, I didn't even hear Grandma come in until she was standing right near me, telling me to turn it down. Sean jumped off the couch and hugged her. I nearly jumped into her arms.

"If you all don't get off me and let me get my coat off, somebody's gonna feel my Bible," Grandma said. "I heard that music down the street!" But she was smiling as she turned the radio off.

Is it still real cold out? Sean signed. *It was freezing earlier.*

"He said, is it cold—"

"I know a little something," Grandma said, cutting me off. She nodded at Sean. She always said she was too old to learn another language by the time Sean came along, but most times, when I tried to translate, she already knew what Sean was signing. And she had a way of signing back that only her and Sean understood most of the times—a kind of secret language that just about burned me up.

She bent down to kiss me and I took her face in my hands and kissed her nose. She laughed and pushed me away the way she always did. She only had two wrinkles—one running straight across her forehead and one small one just at the top of her nose between her eyes. She didn't have any gray hair like other grandmothers but Mama said it was hidden underneath years and years of blue-black hair dye. I liked the color, though—the way the blue kind of caught you by surprise. I took her hand and pulled her over to the couch. Sean had the other hand.

"Now what's all this fuss about this new one coming?" She was talking to both of us but looking at Sean.

"I'm with you," I said. "Doesn't make the least bit of sense."

"What doesn't make sense is both of you pulling on me like you're still my babies." She moved away from us and took off her coat. "I love y'all both to death," she said, putting it on a chair beside her purse. "But you're a little big to be pulling on me so."

She sat down on the couch heavily and pulled me into her lap. I was way too big for laps. I knew that. But me and my whole family made believe that I wasn't. Grandma put her other arm around Sean.

"What's this I hear about Wilt Chamberlain?" Grandma asked Sean.

Thirty thousand points, Sean signed. He had a huge grin on his face.

"And he's the first black man to score that many?"

He's the first any man! Sean said. *In NBA history.*

"Well, ain't he something," Grandma said.

"Argh, that's nothing. If I was in the NBA, I'd score sixty thousand," I said.

And then you'd wake up, Sean said.

"I don't know what I'm going to do with the two of you," Grandma said.

"Grandma, you know this white cat's in my class now. People calling him Jesus!"

Grandma closed her eyes a moment. "Frannie, some days I have no idea what you're talking about. What *cat*?"

"You know, cat, like person. You call a person a cat."

"Is it a cat or is it a person?" Grandma asked. "Because if it's a person, why are you calling him a cat?"

"Grandma! That's the language! That's what you say. It's the seventies! That's *jive* talk."

Grandma just laughed and looked at me.

"Maybe you should concentrate on learning some English first. Before you start learning *jive talk*. And what's this about Jesus?"

"That's what they call him. Because he looks like Jesus—I mean, that's—"

"You don't want a piece of my Bible on your head, now, do you, Frannie." Grandma's face was starting to twist into the face that wasn't so patient.

"No, ma'am. I'm not the one saying it. It's other cats—I mean kids."

Why would Jesus come to your school, Sean said.

I shrugged. "*I'm* not the one saying! I *told* you that. It's other kids." I started getting mad myself. The trouble with this family was you had to explain too much!

"You know the world's changing, Frannie. I don't want to hear about you messing with that boy just because he's white."

"Oh, just forget about it!" I folded my arms and moved off Grandma's lap.

"Come on back here with your stubborn self," Grandma said, pulling me back. "Don't go getting mad now. You just remember there's a time when each one of us is the different one and when it's our turn, we're always wishing and hoping it was somebody else. You be that somebody else when you see that boy. You be the one to remember."

"I *know* that already," I said, not looking at her. "A million times I know that."

"Good," Grandma said. "That's good. Just keep knowing it."

Our living room was starting to get dark—the gray sky coming in all dim through the big windows behind the couch. We hadn't turned on any lights and the TV was off.

For some reason, we just all three sat for a long time like that without saying anything else. After a while, I felt myself relaxing a little. It felt like there was a hundred million things being said all at the same time. Only you didn't need words or signs or face expressions to say them with. I put my head on Grandma's shoulder. It was warm and soft. She smelled like lavender and coconut hair grease.

I stared out the window. Snow coming down like feathers. *You be the one to remember.*

Sean leaned against Grandma's arm and let out a long sigh. After a while, we all just fell asleep that way.

12

The phone rang early Sunday morning and Mama answered. I'd seen the light flashing but had just walked by it on my way to the bathroom. The light was for Sean—he had his own special kind of phone that let you type in what you were saying and messages came back to you. He didn't spend much time on the phone, though. I heard Mama telling me it was Samantha and I picked up the extension phone in the hallway.

"My daddy said it's okay if you come to his church today," Samantha said.

I had tried to remember when I'd asked to go and couldn't come up with the conversation. For some reason, Samantha thought going to church was a treat, like getting a second dessert. I wasn't with her on that.

"I think I don't want to come out in all this snow," I said. I looked up at the picture of Lila on the hallway wall. In the photo, she looked stunned, like she couldn't believe someone was taking her picture. Mama always said it was the camera flash—that Lila hated it. But to me, it looked like she was just surprised to be in this world.

Casper the Friendly Ghost was on the television. He was always trying to get people not to be afraid of him, but it never worked. In the end, they always discovered he was a ghost and went screaming. And Casper always went away sad. But then the next time, he was hopeful again. And then sad again. It went on and on like that. It made me think of the Jesus Boy. The way people kind of stayed away from him just because. I leaned back against the wall and imagined him running after us, yelling, "But I'm a *friendly* ghost!" But just as I was thinking it, the person yelling became Sean and it wasn't funny anymore.

"I was planning on just staying home and watching cartoons," I said. "You know I don't be going for that church jive." I tried to sound cool saying it, but it came out like I was reading or something. Didn't matter. Samantha ignored it anyway.

"You don't have *one* day for God," Samantha said, trying to sound like a grown-up.

"I guess not. I have *one* day for Casper the Friendly Ghost, though."

Samantha knew the worst thing she could do was to try to preach to me.

"You know what I dreamed last night?" she said, and didn't wait for me to answer. "I dreamed I was sitting in God's lap. Isn't that the strangest thing?"

"Well, you must have spent the whole time looking up because Mama says I have a place right on God's shoulder."

Samantha got quiet, and I knew she was standing in her kitchen getting all puffed-up and mad.

"It's not like it's a contest, Samantha," I said after a long time had passed.

"Like what's a contest?"

"Being holy. It's not like whichever cat's the most holiest wins or something."

"Nobody said it was."

I wanted to say "Nobody had to," but didn't. Instead I wrapped the phone cord around my finger and waited for Samantha to say something else.

"Don't you want to be saved, Frannie," Samantha finally asked me.

"You always ask me that and I always say no because you can't even tell me what I'd want to be saved from."

"Yes—I do. I tell you if you get saved, you don't have to worry after you die."

"Yeah, Samantha, but that doesn't make any sense to me because once I die, I'll be done and I won't be worrying anyway."

Now Samantha took a deep breath. And staring at the picture of Lila, hanging on the wall with her eyes all dark and wide, it dawned on me—I wasn't afraid of dying because dying had always been somewhere in our house, somewhere so close, we could feel the wind of it on our cheeks. Lila had died. The other babies had died. And now Mama was pregnant again and maybe this one would make it and maybe it wouldn't. But if it didn't, it would hurt for a while and then we'd figure out how to move on. Samantha was afraid of that—afraid of the feeling of having to move on. She had never had to before, she'd never even known anybody close to her who died. And because of that, the idea of it scared her more than anything. It made me feel a little bit sorry for the people who didn't know much about death.

"You know something, Samantha?"

"What," she answered, sounding all mad.

"Last night I was sitting with my grandma and I was look-ing over her shoulder at the snow coming down. And it made me think about you."

"The snow?"

"Not the snow," I said. "The feeling. It felt holy. All peace-ful and quiet. All promising. It made me think that must be what you feel when you stand in the school yard reading your Bible or sit in your daddy's church listening to him promise the whole congregation . . . something . . . something better coming along."

"Yeah," Samantha said. "When I'm sitting there, it's like there's not anything else in the whole world. Just me and God and heaven. You remember that time you came to my house and we were having corn bread and greens and you asked where the chicken was?"

I nodded. Then I said, "Yes." I'd been so embarrassed when I left Samantha's house that day. There wasn't any chicken because there hadn't been any money for chicken. But I didn't know that until I got home and Mama explained.

"When I go to church, it's like there's always some chicken there, you know. Or steak or roast beef or pork chops or fried fish. It's like there's always something there to go with the greens and the corn bread."

I had gone to school the next day and apologized to Saman-tha, but she'd just said, *Forget about it, there'll be chicken on Fri-day when my mama gets paid. You could come for dinner then if you want to.* And that next Friday I went to her house and ate her mama's baked chicken and we'd never talked about it again. Until now.

"If you want me to go to church with you, Samantha, I'll go," I said, sorry I'd gotten so mad with her.

"Can you come to church with me, Frannie?" Samantha asked, her voice so soft it was hard to hear. "Just 'cause I want you to."

I let out a breath. "Yeah," I said. "I guess so."

Samantha's father's church sat between a Laundromat and a diner. And just like the diner and the Laundromat, his church was a storefront. ONEPEOPLE was written on the big glass window and under that it said REVEREND JOSEPH H. BROWN in gold letters. Before it became a church, OnePeople had been a candy store and hanging above the window was a rusty sign that said DRINK NEHI.

As we drove to OnePeople, Samantha's father talked on and on about how the church was growing.

"God has his hand on my arm," he said, smiling while Samantha's mother nodded. "He's leading me to a bigger church, a better place."

"Amen," Samantha's mother said softly.

I stared out the window, watching the snow coming down. Mama had combed my hair for me so, underneath my hat, I had four cornrows going from front to back. When she'd finished, she'd held my face in her hands and kissed my forehead. "Glad Samantha can get you to church, because Lord knows we can't," she said. Then in the same breath she said, "Is she making you go? Because you know you don't have to."

"I know. I *want* to."

Mama stared into my face. After a minute had passed she said, "When I go to church, I come out feeling good—like there's some reasons to keep on going."

"But I thought me and Sean and Daddy are the reasons you keep on going."

She thought for a moment. "You are, boo. But it's more than that. I feel . . . I feel hopeful. Church makes me remember that tomorrow's always going to be just a little bit better than today."

I nodded.

"So that's why I go. And that's why I ask you and Sean to go sometimes. But I don't know why you want to go today. With Samantha. You know I don't like her daddy's church."

Mama stroked my hair. Her hand felt good.

I wanted to say, *Because Samantha saw the real Jesus in the Jesus Boy and maybe I wanted to see that too.* I wanted to tell Mama that Samantha always seemed to be walking around all hopeful and sure of the something better coming. I wanted to tell Mama about the boy's eyes, how they took in every single thing and didn't change.

"Because Samantha asked me to," I said. I pulled my coat on and the rabbit fur hat Daddy had brought home for me. The hat had long straps with rabbit fur pom-poms at the end. Mama tied the straps beneath my chin and kissed me on the forehead.

"That's as good a reason as any," she said.

I was getting hot inside all that rabbit fur and wool, but I wasn't ready to leave yet.

"Remember when I told you about the poem Ms. Johnson read us?"

Mama smiled. "Yeah, baby. I remember."

"I guess the writer was thinking about how light feathers are and they can just float everywhere. And I guess that's how hope is too—all light and everywhere like that. There's hope in this house. And at your church. And at OnePeople. At our school. Across the highway *and* on this side too. Everywhere."

Mama's eyes got kind of shiny, but she kept on smiling. Then she leaned down and hugged me. Hard.

She got up, put her hand against her mouth. I saw one tear slide down before she turned away from me and walked real fast down the hall. I heard her bedroom door close.

The weekend doorman called up and said, "Someone is here for you."

Samantha's father pulled up in front of his church and smiled. I took Samantha's hand and squeezed it and she looked puzzled for a minute, then she smiled too. And when she smiled, I saw the hope there—the way her eyes got soft, the way her hand wrapped itself around mine . . . and held on.

13

Monday morning, as me and Sean walked to school, two girls came up to us. One of the girls smiled at Sean and said, "What do you know good, pretty boy?" Sean's hair was starting to get longer and that morning he'd picked it out into a short Afro. He was wearing a black turtleneck and his black peacoat, jeans and new boots. Earlier that morning, Mama had smiled at him, saying *You look like one of the Black Panthers,* and Sean had given her the Black Power sign.

"Huh, pretty boy?" the girl said again. "You with the pretty hair and eyes."

I didn't know if I was more shocked by what she was saying or by the fact that they had just come up on us like that. I mean, girls looked at Sean all the time. And sometimes he tried to talk to them. But nobody had ever just walked up to us like that. And what if I had been his girlfriend? But Sean just smiled at her.

"You gonna tell a sister your name?" the girl asked. Her friend giggled but didn't say anything. Sean looked at me and signed, *Tell them.*

"His name is Sean," I said, not very loud either because I didn't feel like being a translator to a girl who thought she could come out of nowhere and say all kinds of things to my brother.

"What's wrong with *his* mouth?" the girl said, rolling her eyes at me.

I wanted to lie and say, "What's wrong with *your* ignorant mouth?" but Sean was looking all happy about the girl, so I didn't. "He's deaf. Just deaf. Not stupid."

Sean made the sign of being deaf—his pointer finger moving from his ear to his mouth.

The girl looked from me to him, then at me again.

"He can't talk either?"

"He just did," I said, getting mad. "You just didn't understand what he said. He said the same thing I just said." I put my hands on my hips, like I was daring her to walk away.

"At least you don't gotta worry about him arguing with you and stuff like that," the girl's friend said to her. "That's what kind of boyfriend *I* need. Somebody who's gonna just be quiet and let me talk."

I signed to Sean, *They're stupid. Even though I know you think she's cute, don't even waste your time. She seems dumber than a broken stick.*

"So, like, if me and him went out," the girl was saying. "You'd have to come with us or something?"

See, I said to Sean. *Can we go now?*

I just looked at the girl.

She grabbed her friend's arm and started walking away. "Dang," she said. "All that fineness wasted."

I could see the smile starting to fall off of Sean's face.

There're lots of pretty deaf girls at your school, I said to Sean. *Why even bother with hearing ones.*

Sean looked away from me. *I know that*, he signed, getting annoyed like it was *my* fault those girls were walking away.

So why do you get all excited when the hearing ones try to talk to you. You know it's going to end up stupid.

Sean shrugged, still looking away. I wondered if he was just ignoring me. But when he started signing again, his hands moved real slowly, like he was trying to make sure I understood.

Remember the bridge?

I shook my head.

You know. When we were sitting at the window that day and I said what if we could build some kind of bridge from every window.

I nodded, slowly remembering.

It's like that, Frannie. The hearing girls are the bridges. They're the other worlds. They're the worlds I can't just walk across and into, you know.

Kind of.

I mean, the deaf girls, they're my world—we don't even have to talk and we know each other. But I don't just want my world. I want everybody else's world too.

But they're just some dumb old girls.

That day, when I said it, you just kind of looked at me like I was crazy. And you know why? Sean looked at me and waited.

Yes, I signed. *Because I didn't understand what you were talking about.*

Yeah. Because you already have both worlds, Frannie. You can walk wherever you want.

14

When Trevor came back to school on Monday, he'd written NY KNICKS all over his cast and wouldn't let anybody write anything else.

"You ain't messing up the Knicks!" he said, standing in the school yard like he was the king of it with his broken-up arm all crossed and all.

"Knicks already messed up," Chris said. "Even the Cavaliers beat them."

"Yeah—for the first time in history," Trevor said.

"Still got their butts beat. I'm trading all my Knicks cards for Cavaliers. You got any?" Chris took a stack of basketball cards out of his pocket and held them out to Trevor.

Trevor scowled down at the cards and said, "Man, you better get out of my face."

Lots of people had been mad when the Knicks got beat by the Cavaliers. Even though it was the first time in the history of basketball, people lost their minds. Sean read every single sports page he could get his hands on.

Everything is changing, he'd said, looking a little lost.

It had snowed all weekend and the school yard looked like something out of a picture. Over where the little kids played, the jungle gym and slide and everything was all covered in white. Later on, they'd come outside and their tiny little feet would leave dirty prints everywhere. But now, it was just beautiful, the sky so bright over everything you had to shield your eyes. I stood there looking up at the sky, thinking about what Sean had said that morning. When we got to the place where he turned off to go to Daffodil, he punched me gently on the shoulder and signed, *I don't care about those dumb old girls.* But he was lying and we both knew it. I watched him walk away, all dressed like a Black Panther but looking a little bit smaller than when we'd left the house that morning.

I didn't see the Jesus Boy come into the school yard until he was standing right near us, his hands in his pockets, his pale face turned up toward the sky, his long hair hanging all curly down his back. He saw me looking and waved. Samantha waved back.

The pocks on my palms itched. Whenever I scratched them, I thought about the sign for Jesus—the middle finger of one hand brushing over the palm of the other.

Maribel came over to us and stood next to Samantha. I rolled my eyes. She was wearing a new pair of platform boots—the shiny leather kind with the buckle. When I'd asked Mama if I could get them, she'd given me a look and said, *You can't even walk right in flat shoes!*

"A penny for your thoughts, Jesus Boy," Maribel said.

When me and Samantha didn't laugh, she said, "Well, that's all that boy seems to have. He came in with some more on Saturday. They must have a penny garden in their yard or something."

"Copper's supposed to be good for dirt," I said.

Maribel made a face but Samantha smiled.

Jesus Boy walked slowly, his head still kind of lifted a bit. He went and stood by the fence. After a few minutes, Trevor and all of them went over to him.

"You still here?" Trevor said.

The Jesus Boy looked down at his boots. He was wearing a new-looking blue peacoat that was a little too big for him.

"You hear a brother talking to you?" Trevor said.

The Jesus Boy looked up again and sort of shrugged.

"Rayray, you think this white cat's—"

"Leave him alone, Trev," Rayray said, his voice trembling a bit. "He ain't messing with us."

"Rayray's talking back to Trevor?" Maribel whispered. "You know it must be snowing."

But Samantha smiled. "He's taking up for Jesus Boy. Bible says when Jesus Christ came back, there were miracles everywhere."

"Nah," I said. "I think he just lost his mind. He was always a little bit crazy, so it's not some miracle or anything."

Trevor turned to Rayray. "I know you ain't trying to tell me what to do now." He tapped his ear with his good hand. "I just know that ain't what I'm hearing."

"Why you gotta be so . . . so mad all the time, Trev," Rayray said, taking a step back.

Trevor was quiet for a moment; he looked a little bit confused. Then he shook his head, laughed and turned back to the Jesus Boy.

Me and Samantha and Maribel stood shivering across from

86

them. For some reason, I knew something was coming that I didn't want to see. I saw the way Trevor's face got angry again when he talked to the Jesus Boy. I saw the way the other kids were starting to move in closer.

"Well, it's just a bit too cold out here for me," I said to Samantha. "I'm heading inside." But just as I started walking away from them, I heard Trevor curse the Jesus Boy and tell him to throw up his hands. I turned back then.

The one fight I'd ever had was back in second grade. A boy whose name I didn't remember anymore had tried to take the money Mama had given me for an after-school snack. The boy didn't get the money—he'd knocked me down and I'd kicked him hard in the knee. I didn't like fighting. Not seeing them. Not having them. After I'd had that fight, even though nothing really hurt and I still had my money, I cried and cried and cried.

Jesus Boy stood there. He had a long red string of licorice wrapped around his finger. "Why do you want to fight me, Trevor?" he said, then put the licorice in his mouth and chewed slowly, not taking his eyes off of him. "Is it because I have a daddy? And you don't?"

I stopped dead. Nobody talked about Trevor's daddy. The whole school yard seemed to get quiet. Some of the kids said, "Oooh."

"I know this cat ain't say what I thought he said." Trevor took a step closer to the Jesus Boy.

"You heard me right," the Jesus Boy said quietly, but there was a hardness inside the quiet that made me shiver even more. I watched the Jesus Boy's face. It seemed so calm, like it knew some next thing was coming and was more than ready for it.

"White boy, you must—"

"I ain't your white boy," the Jesus Boy said. "You color-blind?" He stepped away from the fence. A step closer to Trevor. Trevor didn't back up, though.

I took a deep breath. I couldn't believe he was standing up there, trying to tell them he wasn't white. Even if he did have a brown daddy, there wasn't anything about him that looked Not White.

"Yeah," Chris said. "He's spirit-colored. Ain't that right, Rayray?"

Rayray just stared at the Jesus Boy like the rest of us—trying to find the Not White part of him.

Standing there in the snow, with all those kids standing around, it came to me—his calmness, his hair, the paleness of his skin—he'd always had to walk through the world this way, push through. Maybe he'd met a whole bunch of Trevors in his life. Maybe he'd go on meeting them.

"My mama isn't white and my daddy isn't white and as far as I know it, you're the one with the white daddy living across the highway." He took another step toward Trevor, but even as he said those words, his voice stayed quiet. But then I looked at his hand, watched it close into a fist.

"I saw his daddy on Saturday," I whispered to Samantha. "He's brown like us brown. Not even light-skinned."

Samantha's eyes went wide, then she frowned, trying to figure it out.

"I bet that isn't his real father," she said after a while. "The way Joseph wasn't really Jesus' father."

"Girl," Maribel said. "This world is just too many things."

"Okay, Miss Parrot," I said. "Did you hear your mama or your grandma say that?"

"I heard *your* mama say it."

"Don't talk about my mama," I said.

"Shush, y'all," Samantha said. "Enough fights in this school yard already." She closed her eyes a moment and I knew it was to pray silently. When she opened them again, the Jesus Boy's hand was still in a fist, opening and closing. Opening and closing.

I looked at Trevor standing there, his face looking like it was trying to figure out what to do next. I looked at his broken arm. At the cast climbing all the way up to his shoulder, at the way his too-small coat couldn't quite cover it. The fence in the park faced the highway. Maybe he'd hoped he could jump and keep on jumping—through the sky and across the highway, on and on until he landed right back in his daddy's arms.

And maybe because Trevor didn't have anything to say back to the Jesus Boy, maybe that's why he took a swing at him with that one good arm, missing and stumbling, then falling. And maybe because Trevor had always been on the evil side, maybe that's why kids starting laughing when he fell, instead of running to him and helping him up out of the snow.

"You *crying*, man?" Rayray said. He looked confused and surprised. He was standing just a few feet away from his friend. But he didn't move toward Trevor. Didn't try to lift him up out of the snow. "I can't believe you're *crying*," he said.

"I ain't crying!"

I went to Trevor. The minute I saw him falling, I went toward him. It was automatic. Something inside me just said, "Go!" And I did. Because Trevor was falling and then he was in the snow. And in the snow he looked smaller and weaker and more human than any of us. When I looked up, the Jesus Boy was on the other side of me. And we were both lifting Trevor even as he tried to shake us off him and keep from crying.

Then Trevor was standing again. Standing but cursing both of us. But his curse words sounded strange—hollow and far-away. Like he was just learning them. Like he was practicing at being some kind of tough kid. Instead of truly being one.

Then he just stopped cursing and stood there, his head hanging down, his one good hand in his pocket. He didn't look like Trevor anymore. Standing there all pale and sad and shivering, he looked like he was somebody else.

15

Hope is the thing with feathers. After Ms. Johnson had read us that poem, she asked us why we thought the poet wrote that. Trevor was the one who had said, *Maybe because she wanted to fly.*

Like a feathered bird, he'd said. And then he went back to staring out the window.

Or maybe, I'd said, *because, like those yucky pigeons, hope is always all around us.*

As me and the Jesus Boy walked away from Trevor, I saw Samantha watching us as we headed into the school building.

"Hey," Rayray said, coming up behind us. "Y'all okay?"

"He's fine," I said, thinking he was asking about Trevor.

"Not Trevor. You. You and JB." I turned then. He was looking at me—his face softer and more serious than I'd ever seen it before.

Jesus Boy smiled and shrugged.

"We're cool, Rayray," I said. "Why you asking?"

"I ain't scared of Trevor anymore," Rayray said. "I'm not going to let him hit me in the head anymore either. I bet none of us gonna be scared of him. He's just like us. Just a kid. You don't need to be scared of no kid." He looked at the Jesus Boy.

"You all right, my man," he said, giving the Jesus Boy the Power sign. "You think you gonna stay at Price?"

Jesus Boy took another piece of licorice out of his pocket, put half of it into his mouth and chewed slowly. He looked calmly over the school yard. "Don't have no place else to go," he said. "Gotta stay."

"I hear that," Rayray said. "This is the end of the line." Then he turned away from us, did a Michael Jackson spin, winked at us, said, "Or the beginning. Or *something*." And walked off again.

I looked over to where Trevor was standing. He was still there, leaning against the school yard fence now, his good hand still stuffed in his pocket. He shivered and stared up into the falling snow.

"Look how fast," I said. "One minute you're one thing." I snapped my finger. "The next minute you're another."

And the Jesus Boy stared at Trevor, then looked down at his own hands. "The bad thing is, a part of me wants to go over there and hit him and just keep on hitting him, you know."

"Why?"

Jesus Boy shrugged. "Just because. Because I could do it and everybody would probably cheer. Everybody would think I'm some kind of hero. I could be the new Trevor around here—with people being scared of me and all. It would be that easy."

"But then," I said, "who'd Trevor be?"

The Jesus Boy thought for a minute. "He'd be me," he said. "Trevor would be the Jesus Boy."

Jesus wept, Samantha had said. That was the shortest verse in the Bible. But Jesus hadn't wept. Trevor had. Jesus had seen something other kids hadn't seen. Not because they couldn't. Because their hearts were kinder. But the Jesus Boy had gone right to the soft hurting spot in Trevor. And he'd peeled the skin of that hurting back to show us all the scar that was there.

Jesus hurt somebody.

And the hurting proved to all of us that the Jesus Boy was just a boy. A white-black boy. A human boy all complicated and crazy as the rest of us.

He wasn't no Wilt Chamberlain or Cleveland Cavalier or Neil Armstrong taking the first step on the moon.

And all the other kids had seen it. Had seen the way Trevor fell. Had seen the tears. Had seen, in that quick, quick moment, how small we all could be.

Jesus Boy held the door open for me and I let him. When we were inside, we headed to Ms. Johnson's class just as the bell rang, signaling the beginning of another day.

16

Most of the way home that afternoon, me and Samantha were quiet. The snow was coming down in heavy white flakes and the snow on the ground came up past my ankles. We walked slowly through it, afraid of slipping on the patches of ice beneath the snow. That afternoon in geography, we had talked about weather in different parts of the world. It was hard to think that in some places, the sun was shining and people were walking half-naked along beaches. Because even though Ms. Johnson said that in other places crocuses were blooming and kids were jumping into bright blue swimming pools, right here, where we were, it was still winter. It felt like it would always be.

"You ever think spring's gonna come?"

Samantha shrugged. She looked down as she walked, taking high careful steps through the snow. "It always did before, didn't it?"

We walked awhile longer without talking. When we finally got to where we went in different directions, Samantha turned to me.

"He's just a regular old boy, isn't he?" she said. "The Jesus Boy. He's just regular."

I nodded. "But he seems nice, right?"

"He would have hit Trevor if it had come to that," Samantha said. She took a deep breath and looked out past me to where the highway was. The cars moved slowly along, the snow muffling the sound. Far off, I could hear a low whistle—like wind moving toward us from somewhere far away.

"Strange," Samantha said. "How one day you can believe in something. And the next day you don't anymore." She shivered. There was a hole in one of her mittens. When she saw me looking at it, she put her hand in her pocket.

"And then, when you don't have that thing to believe in anymore, you don't have *anything*."

Then, without saying anything else, she turned and started walking away from me. I watched her go, not knowing what to say.

PART FOUR

17

By the time I got home on Monday, it was snowing again, coming down in big, wet flakes. The heat was blasting when I opened the front door of our apartment and I rushed inside. I could smell something good cooking and ran into the kitchen without even taking my shoes off. Mama was standing at the stove, chicken grease popping loud and heating up the kitchen.

"Girl, you must have lost your mind," Mama said. "If you don't get back out there and take off those boots, you better! And get some paper towels and wipe up that trail you trying to leave through my house."

I smiled, hugged her and went back down the hall.

"You feeling all better, Ma?"

Mama didn't say anything. I got my boots and coat off quick as anything and ran back into the kitchen, then grabbed some paper towels and started wiping. "You look all better. Huh, Mama? You feeling all better, because you look—"

"I'm standing here making this chicken, right?"

I nodded, looking up at her and smiling.

"Well, that must account for something, huh?"

"Accounts for Mr. Hungry calling that chicken's name."

Mama smiled and leaned over to kiss me on the cheek. "Remember when Mr. Hungry moved into your brain, girl?"

I thought about it and frowned. "I don't even remember," I said. "I've always said that."

"Since you were about five—the first time you saw a commercial for those biscuits. The one that said, *There's a hungry man inside of everyone!*" Mama laughed. "You got so scared that there was some man living inside of you. It took me and your father about an hour to calm you down. That's when Mr. Hungry moved into this apartment."

I tried to remember the commercial she was talking about but couldn't remember a single minute of it.

Mama had the radio on. A group called the 5th Dimension was singing, *"Then peace will guide the planets. And love will steer the stars . . ."*

I leaned against the counter. "Mama . . ."

Mama was reaching up to get some plates down. Her belly was tiny and round now.

She stopped reaching and turned to me. "What, honey," she asked, her eyes looking all worried. Maybe it was the way I'd called her.

"It's so strange, isn't it? The way some things stay in our memory and other things don't. Like I don't remember any of that—not even the commercial. Where does all that memory go to?"

Mama checked her chicken, then turned the heat down underneath the pan.

She folded her arms and leaned against the sink. "It's there inside of us somewhere. It comes up in other ways, I guess. Like even though you don't have the memory, you got Mr. Hungry." She smiled.

I thought about how hurt Sean had looked this morning.

"Does stuff go away?"

Mama sighed and turned back to her chicken. "I don't think the important stuff does," she said. "You know—the stuff that really makes an impression. I don't think you remember it just as it happened—but you remember the feelings you had. Good ones. And bad ones too, unfortunately."

"Hmmm . . ."

Mama looked over her shoulder at me. "How about we make a good memory right now and you get those potatoes mashed, baby girl." She pointed to the bowl of potatoes on the table. I threw the paper towels away, got a fork from the drawer and started pressing it into the potatoes.

"How about giving those hands a quick washing?"

"I was wearing gloves, Ma!"

"Not when you were wiping up that snow water, you weren't."

Our old mama's returned, I signed behind her back, then headed to the bathroom.

The minute I started working the potatoes, the door slammed. After a few minutes, Sean was standing there watching us, his face broken out in this huge smile. I tried to see some memory of those dumb girls and found it—just a little bit, right around his eyes, they weren't real bright, even though he was smiling.

We're having chickennnnnnn, we've having chickennnnn, I signed, moving my hand slowly at the end of the word *chicken* and doing a little dance. Sean's smile got a little bigger.

What'd the doctor say? Sean asked. He sure knew how to kill a moment!

Took some tests, Mama signed. She pulled some chicken thighs out of the hot oil with a fork and laid them on a flattened paper bag she had put next to the stove. *Said the baby's looking just fine.*

And she's feeling good right now, I signed, glaring at Sean. *That's what matters.*

Sean tapped his head with his hand and made a face at me, which basically translated into *I see that, stupid.*

I didn't care. Mama was cooking, we were having chicken and mashed potatoes and greens and Mr. Hungry was gonna be packing his bags *to-night!*

18

The next morning, the Jesus Boy came up to me just as we were lining up to go inside. He looked like he wanted to say something, then just looked down at the ground. After a moment, he raised his head again.

"I probably shouldn't have talked about his daddy, huh?"

I shrugged. "I don't know. I mean, he was saying stuff about you. I never understood why you let him say and do all those mean things to you in the first place. Didn't make any sense."

We stood there. Somebody had a transistor radio going and I could hear little pieces of the Jackson 5 song "I'll Be There." Across the school yard, I could see a group of girls moving slowly to the music.

On the news that morning, they'd talked about a draft lottery to get more guys signed up for the war that was going on and Mama had stopped frying bacon and kissed *both* of Sean's ears.

Jesus Boy looked at me. Some days, he looked real beautiful—the way the bones in his face kinda pushed out against his pale skin, the way his gray eyes looked all these other colors when the sun came near them.

"It frees him," he said. "All that stuff that makes him mad and mean and ugly leaves him when he does stuff to other people."

"Until the next time," I said. "Then it all just comes right back."

The sun went behind some clouds and the wind picked up. I shivered.

"But maybe the next time, it'll be a little bit less and a little bit less and a little bit less until it's finally all gone." He looked up at the sky—like he was trying to see the wind. I looked up too—trying to see what he saw. Just the graying sky. Just the snow starting to come down again.

Trevor came up behind the Jesus Boy and made a face at his back. Then he moved between us.

"I want to introduce y'all," Trevor said, pointing at me. "To Mrs. Jesus." Some kids laughed. I saw Rayray flick his eyes at Trevor.

"Come on off it already, Trev," I heard him say. "It's getting tired. That boy ain't doing nothing to you. Frannie ain't either."

"Jesus loves me, this I know," Trev sang softly as he started walking away again.

Rayray just turned away from him and headed inside the building.

A little bit less and a little bit less. I guess calling me Mrs. Jesus wasn't the meanest thing Trevor could say.

When we got inside the school, Ms. Johnson was in the hallway, talking to another teacher. As we walked quietly into the classroom, I saw her looking at Jesus Boy.

"Let's start with some writing this morning," she said. Most of the class groaned. I just took out my notebook and let it make a loud slap on my desk, liking the sound it made.

"No slamming books," Ms. Johnson said, looking at me. "We write in books, we read books—we don't slam books. If you're mad, go home and slam a door, please."

The sun was out and melting snow dripped down over the windows.

"Now what we're going to do this morning," she said, her voice becoming all bright again. "Is write down the things we all have in common. I love this exercise because the lists are always so different, which means"—she stopped and looked around the room—"this is not the time to discuss your list with each other. Just write."

She was wearing a pretty blue dress with black platform boots that came just below her knee. Ms. Johnson always looked like she'd spent the whole weekend looking through fashion magazines, then going out and buying whatever was in style. Samantha would probably grow up to be like Ms. Johnson because she dressed nice too. I usually put on whatever was clean and sometimes that didn't amount to much. Mama said one day I'd care a little more about how I looked, but I didn't see that day coming in the near future.

"Rayray, Trevor, Maribel and Chris," Ms. Johnson said. "The answers aren't outside that window."

Maribel rolled her eyes like she was insulted that Ms. Johnson had the nerve to say something to her. Everybody else just faced front.

I stared down at my blank notebook page, wondering what to write. Here's the list I came up with.

- We all go to Price.
- We all wear clothes.
- All of us kids live on this side of the highway.
- We all walked in the snow at least once this winter. Maybe a hundred times.

I looked around the classroom. Rayray was slumped down in his chair. Trevor had gone back to staring out the window. The Jesus Boy's pen was moving real slow over his paper. I thought about the way all of our mamas and daddies must have looked at us when we were babies—all new to the world, all squishy-faced and spider-fingered, and them loving us anyway. I thought about my own mama—the way she smiled at me sometimes like she couldn't believe I was her daughter.

- We were all little babies one time.

19

On Wednesday morning, Maribel was absent, so Samantha and me got to sit alone at lunchtime. The cafeteria was loud and hot. We were having that goulash thing for lunch again.

"Frannie," Samantha said. "I got something I've been wanting to ask you."

I looked up at her.

"That day—when Trevor and Jesus Boy had that fight? How come you went over to him?"

Samantha was wearing a blue suede vest over a turtleneck. She had dangly earrings in her ears and had gotten her hair cornrowed. I leaned on my fist and stared at her. We'd been friends for so many years, I'd stopped counting. She was one of the few people outside my family who knew about the pock scars on my hand. When I'd showed them to her, all those years ago, she was the one who'd said, "Those could be nail holes."

"It was the right thing," I said softly.

Samantha took a small bite of the cracker that came with the goulash and kept looking at me.

"You know—Trevor was on the ground, looking like he was going to cry. And then, maybe you couldn't see it, but he *was* crying. And he was having a hard time getting up with his

arm and all . . ." I stopped talking because I realized I was talking real fast. Until that moment, I hadn't really understood
why I went over to him.

"But Trevor's always been so mean," Samantha said.

Now I just looked at her.

"I don't know why you'd help someone so mean like that,"
she said.

"Because he needed it," I said. "I don't know. I'd even help
Maribel get up if she fell down. I don't really like her but—I
don't know. It's what you *do*."

"But you don't even hardly go to church," Samantha said.

I picked up one of the crackers, then put it down again. Mr.
Hungry wasn't anywhere to be found anymore. I couldn't believe I had to explain what I didn't know how to explain. I'd
figured Samantha would just understand—deep inside. Of
all people.

"It was the right thing," I said again. "Trevor was just sitting there in the snow."

"And why do you think the Jesus Boy went over to him?"
Samantha asked. But she wasn't looking at me. She was looking over at the Jesus Boy. "I mean, you know—after he said
those bad things about Trevor's dad?" She frowned. "After he
showed his true colors and all. And me thinking that maybe
he'd come here really being Jesus and all."

I looked at Samantha. "Maybe he is," I said.

"You're crazy. Jesus would never say something about
somebody's daddy."

"But he wept," I said. "You said so yourself. And so did
Trevor. So maybe Trevor's Jesus!"

"That's blasphemy," Samantha said.

"I was hoping . . . ," she said slowly. "I was hoping so hard that Jesus had come back and had come right into our classroom. And the hoping turned into believing, I guess." She put her head on her fist and stared at the Jesus Boy. "But Rayray was right. Why would Jesus come *here,* to this side of the highway, to Price."

"But he did, Samantha. The Jesus Boy did."

"But he's not the real Jesus."

"Maybe he is. Maybe there's a little bit of Jesus inside of all of us. Maybe Jesus is just that something good or something sad or something . . . something that stays with us and makes us do stuff like help Trevor up even though he's busy cursing us out. Or maybe . . . maybe Jesus is just that thing you had when the Jesus Boy first got here, Samantha. Maybe Jesus is the hope that you were feeling."

"You don't make any kind of sense," Samantha said.

But I did make sense. Maybe I only made sense to me. But maybe I was the only one I *needed* to make sense to.

20

Ms. Johnson says everybody has a story. She said some of us are afraid to tell ours and that's why when it comes time to write something, we say we have writer's block. Ms. Johnson says there's no such thing as writer's block. She said it's just your mind saying to your body, *I ain't trying to write that jive.* Everybody laughed when she said it like that because, mostly, Ms. Johnson speaks proper.

"Then what does your mind want your hand to write?" Ms. Johnson asked the class.

Trevor was tracing the letters on his desk. Rayray was staring out the window. I looked down at my blank paper, my pencil in my hand and my hand and mind real still and quiet.

"Frannie?" Ms. Johnson looked at me.

I shrugged. "A story?"

"Maybe," Ms. Johnson said. She walked slowly over to Rayray and turned his head gently toward the front of the room. She walked over to Trevor, lifted his pencil out of his hand.

"If the story is the truth," Ms. Johnson said.

"But that's nonfiction then," somebody said.

"The truth in your heart. My daddy says we all have a truth in our hearts."

It was the Jesus Boy speaking. He even surprised Ms. Johnson. But she tried to hide it by smiling.

"Exactly," Ms. Johnson said. "Write what your heart tells you to write."

We all looked around the room at each other. Nobody said anything.

"My heart's not saying *anything*," Rayray said. He slumped down in his chair. "I *hate* this."

Ms. Johnson walked back to the front of the room. "Think of a day in your life," she said. "Any kind of day—where something big happened or nothing at all happened. Something important or something just regular, like you ate a sandwich while watching some cartoons. *Anything*. Just try to write down every single detail you can remember about it."

The Jesus Boy raised his hand. "When I was three years old, my mama and daddy brought me home and told me that they'd be my mama and daddy from that point on—"

I heard someone whisper, "So that's it! He's adopted!" but the Jesus Boy didn't hear. Or maybe he ignored them.

"And from then on, that was my mom and that was my dad. But I don't remember anything about that day, so how can I write it?"

Ms. Johnson nodded. "That's an excellent question. How do we write what we don't remember."

We all just looked at her.

"How about," she said slowly. "How about *imagining* how something felt." She turned back to the Jesus Boy. "Imagine how that day must have felt for you," she said.

And slowly, the Jesus Boy smiled as though all the memory was suddenly flooding back into his brain.

I looked down at my paper. There were a million days in my head, all of them marching all over each other. All of them coming from my heart and feeling like my heart-truth. I didn't have the slightest idea where to begin. There were all kinds of thoughts swirling around in my head and it felt like the whole class dropped away and disappeared and all that was left was me and my pen and my paper and the whole wide world spinning around me. I felt dizzy with all those thoughts, had to put my head down on the desk.

"Frannie, are you okay?" I heard Ms. Johnson asking. Her voice sounded like it was coming from real far away.

I nodded into my arm but didn't lift my head. "I don't even know what the first line to write would be," I said.

"Begin at Frannie's beginning," Ms. Johnson said.

The first word I ever learned was *now*. Sean said I was not even two years old when he showed me the word—middle fingers against your palms, thumbs and pinkies up and your hands moving down.

I lifted my head and took a deep breath.

My brother taught me to speak, I wrote. *I grew up inside his world of words . . .*

21

That afternoon, as Samantha and me walked home, the Jesus Boy came running up to us. Samantha looked at him without really looking at him. Now that she'd discovered he wasn't really Jesus, it was like she couldn't care less about him.

"Hey," the Jesus Boy said.

"Hey yourself," I said back.

Samantha just watched us.

"I'm swimming tomorrow," he said. "It's Saturday."

I looked at him and nodded.

"So if you go to the rec center, you'll probably see me." He smiled.

"Okay," I said.

"Okay," he said back. Then none of us said anything.

"I guess I should head home then," the Jesus Boy said.

"Okay," I said again.

He turned, then turned back again. "Hey Frannie," he said. "It would be cool if I saw you there."

For the first time, he didn't look calm. He looked nervous and a little bit scared.

"Maybe it was somebody you knew," I said, signing the words at the same time. "Before your mama and daddy brought you home. Maybe there was somebody who you knew who knew how to sign, right?"

The Jesus Boy smiled. "I remember and I don't remember. That's crazy, right?"

I thought about Mr. Hungry, how he stayed with me even though I didn't remember a single thing about the commercial. "It's not real crazy," I said. "Just a little bit crazy."

Samantha stared at us.

"If you see a empty pinball machine," I said, "get it. And stay on it until I get there." I gave him the peace sign.

The Jesus Boy looked confused for a minute. Then he smiled. Then the smile got a little bit bigger. "See you tomorrow," he said.

Me and Samantha watched him walk away.

"Was he trying to ask you on a date or something?"

I stared at his back.

We started walking again.

"Nah," I said. "He's just a new kid. That's all. Remember when I was the new kid?"

"That was a long time ago," Samantha said.

"You forget a whole lotta stuff by the time you're eleven and a half, Samantha. But you don't forget *that*. It stays with you. Always."

Samantha turned again and watched the Jesus Boy. "It would have been nice, Frannie. It would have meant all that *believing* and *hoping* I do all the time means something, you know." She took my hand. "If he had really been Jesus, that would have been nice."

"Yeah," I said, squeezing her hand. "I would have asked

about Lila—if she was okay. If she was having fun." I looked at Samantha. "And I would have asked about the one that's coming—about all the ones that are coming all over the world . . . I would have asked Him if we were all gonna be all right."

I looked up at the sky and took a deep breath.

"Some days," I said. "I just want to know that we're all gonna be all right."

We walked the rest of the way without talking, Samantha holding tight to my hand.

22

The baby inside Mama's belly grows and grows. This morning, I wake to find her in the rocker by the window, staring out into the sun. She looks beautiful sitting there with all the light around her.

"Hey sleepyhead," she says. "Can you believe this sun? After all those weeks of snow?" She smiles. "Your daddy just went out to get some muffin mix. This one craves the same things you did."

I craved burgers, Sean says. He is in his blue pajamas and has his head against the wall next to the stereo speaker. There is soft music coming out. Sean puts his hand on the speaker and sways. *Just like a true basketball star.*

I don't know what burgers have to do with basketball, but I don't tell Sean.

Everything in the living room is lit up bright gold by the sun. I stand there staring at the way it falls across the couch and the coffee table and Mama in her rocking chair and Sean on the floor beside her.

Ms. Johnson says each day holds its own memory—its own moments that we can write about later. She says we should always look for the moments and some of them might be perfect, filled with light and hope and laughter. Moments that stay with us forever and ever. Amen.

On the stereo, a man with a beautiful high voice is singing about a bridge over troubled water. *When darkness comes,* he sings, *and pain is all around. I will comfort you . . .*

Maybe later, I'll tag along with Sean to the rec center. Maybe I'll watch him play and think of evil things to say to the hearing girls.

Maybe I'll stand in the hall and find some new graffiti on the posters. Maybe I'll beat the Jesus Boy at pinball and be the pinball champion of the world.

I climb onto Mama's lap and put my head against her shoulder, my feet hanging all the way down to the floor. Sean rolls his eyes and signs, *Big baby.* But Mama just laughs and puts her arms around me.

And if Samantha shows up, maybe we can all three hang out together and she can start to see the Jesus inside the boy inside the Jesus Boy.

Maybe.

"Let the baby have some room, Franny," Mama says, shifting a little.

From somewhere inside Mama's belly, a tiny foot kicks at me.

"For a little while longer," I say, "I'm the baby in this family."

"For a little while," Mama says.

And in case you didn't know, Sean says. *A little while isn't long at all.*

I stick my tongue out at him and he laughs.

I know that, I say. *A million times I know that!*

Then I put my head on Mama's shoulder and close my eyes, the sun warm against my face, the man's voice on the record getting softer and higher. Then fading away.

Each moment, I am thinking, *is a thing with feathers.*

ACKNOWLEDGMENTS

With so much love and thanks to Nancy Paulsen, who has always seen the book inside the mess that is the early draft.

Toshi Reagon, Patti Sullivan, Jill Harris, An Na, Valerie Winborne, Jana Welch, Linda Villarosa, Jane Sasseen, Jayme Lynes, patient listeners that you are—thank you.

The young people in Cynthiana, Kentucky, in St. Louis, Missouri, and right here in Brooklyn at New Voices Middle School—thanks for listening.

And thanks also to Toshi G., Omilana, Gus and Jo, Ellison, Tashawn, Kali, Nicky, Juna, Lissa, Baby June, Ming, and Ella. Each day, you are my feathers.

Turn the page for a sample of
Jacqueline Woodson's newest book,

Peace, Locomotion

Imagine peace.

I think it's blue because that's my favorite color.

*I think it's soft like flannel sheets in the
      wintertime.*

*I think Peace is full—
      like a stomach after a real good dinner—
      beef stew and corn bread or
      shrimp fried rice and egg rolls.*

Even better

Than some barbecue chicken.

I think Peace is pretty—like my sister, Lili.

And I think it's nice—like my friend Clyde.

*I think if you imagine it, like that
      Beatles guy used to sing about?*

Then it can happen.

Yeah, I think

Peace Can Happen.

-Lonnie Collins Motion,
aka **Locomotion**

Dear Lili,

As you know, in a few days I'm going to be twelve. That means two things:

1. In six weeks, you'll be nine.
2. In nine more years, I'll be twenty-one and then I'll be old enough to take care of you by myself. And when I'm twenty-one and you're eighteen, I'll still be your big brother and kind of like the boss of you. But I won't be mean. And if you want, we can keep living in Brooklyn. Maybe we'll even find a place near your foster mama's house because I know you like it a lot over there since it's right near the park and there's a cool playground and stuff. When we're together again, I'll take you to that playground myself so you won't be missing it. Even if we're big, we can still go, right? I see big kids at the one over here sometimes. They hang off the jungle gym and go down the slide. They be acting all crazy and having a real good time.

When we were small, Mama used to take us to the playground over by where our old house was. Since you were still real little, she'd have to go with you down the slide. "Lonnie, you take your sister down the slide now," she'd say sometimes.

And even though I felt kind of stupid doing that with my friends there watching and singing, *Lonnie gotta baby-sit, Lonnie gotta baby-sit,* I did it anyways because Mama would get that smile on her face. Daddy used to say, "That's a smile make a regular man climb Kilimanjaro."

Back then, I didn't even know what Kilimanjaro was. Now I do though. It's a mountain in Africa. And if Mama and Daddy were alive and we were still little kids, I'd take you down that slide a hundred times. And climb Kilimanjaro if Mama asked me to.

Love,

Your brother to the
highest mountain,
Locomotion

Dear Lili,

This morning, when I got up and saw the rain still coming down, I sat on the couch watching it for a long, long time, thinking about you and Mama and Daddy. Thinking about when we was all together and we'd do things like take the bus to the Prospect Park Zoo and take the train to Coney Island. Or like when me and Daddy used to go to the Mets games and everybody would always be asking us how come we liked the Mets when the Yankees was the ones always winning. I remember Daddy said, "Ain't it boring to always be winning?" And I thought about that for a long time even though I was just a little kid. I thought about how if you walk out on the field or the basketball court or the handball court already knowing you got the game in the bag, what's the point? Like when me and Angel and Lamont and Clyde be playing ball and we get some in and miss some—well, like when that ball finally goes through that net and you hear that *swoosh!* sound and your homeboys be slapping your back and saying "good shot" and stuff? If you knew that was coming, you wouldn't even get that good feeling you get when it happens. You'd just be all regular and not caring and stuff. But when I was a little kid, I'd just say, "Winning's fun and I *sure* wish the Mets would win a little bit more!" Daddy used to laugh that big laugh of his and hug me so hard I couldn't even feel my breath moving through my lungs.

Felt real good, Lili.

Locomotion

Dear Lili,

Every day, the memories get a little bit more faded out of my head and I try to pull them back. It's like they used to be all colorful and loud and everything. They're getting grayer though. And sometimes even the ones that used to be loud get real, real quiet.

Lili, do you remember? There was a time when all of us were together. There was a time before the fire and before nobody wanted to be my foster mama until Miss Edna came along. There was a time before your foster mama came and said, "I'll take the little girl but I don't want no boys." You were the little girl, Lili. And you didn't want to go. It was raining that day just like it's raining now. And you held on to me and cried and cried. You kept saying, *I want to be with my brother.*

And I hope you know that I wanted to be with you too. But I didn't want you living in a group home anymore. I wanted you in a nice house with nice people and not kids everywhere taking your stuff and being mean to you.

Remember I said, *One day, we'll be together again*? I know that day is taking a lot longer to come than it should, but I still believe it's gonna get here, Little Sister. And that's why I'm trying to write you lots and lots. Because I love writing and I love you and when me and you are together again, I'm gonna want us to remember everything that happened when we were living apart. I'm gonna hold on to all these letters and when we're living together again, they're gonna be the first present I give you. A whole box of the Before Time. That's what this is, Lili, even though I know when me and you get sad, all we think about is the other Before Time—before the fire, before we lived apart from each other. But this is a whole new Before Time. And it's cool, because we'll be able to remember a whole other set of good things, right? So I'm writing. And I'm remembering. For me. And for you, Lili.

Love,

Locomotion

Dear Lili,

I know it's been three years since that day when your foster mama came. But the way I figure it—me and you are both gonna live to be at least a hundred years old and given that fact—three years, four years, even if it takes nine years—well, that's not a real, real long time after all.

Love you to eternity,

Locomotion

Dear Lili,

Today in school we got the good news that Ms. Cooper is going to be leaving soon. Her belly's been growing a lot since school started but nobody in class liked her enough to ask if that was a baby inside. Not even LaTenya and LaTenya likes *everybody*. On the first day of school, I told Ms. Cooper I was a poet since last year Ms. Marcus told me that's what I should call myself because she said my poems were real good. I liked saying *I'm a poet* a whole lot and every time I say it to Rodney or Miss Edna, they always say *You sure are, so just keep on writing those poems, Lonnie.* But when I said it to Ms. Cooper, she just looked at me and folded her arms. Then she asked me if I'd published any books. I said not yet, since I'm only in sixth grade and all. But I told her I wanted to publish a whole lot one day. Ms. Cooper just gave me her back and walked over to her desk. She said, "Until you publish a book, you're not a poet, you're an *aspiring* poet, Lonnie." So after that I went back to being just a regular boy—not a poet like Ms. Marcus had said. I don't think Ms. Marcus had been lying. I guess there's just people that think you're a good poet and people who don't really care about poetry and the people who like to write it. I still write a few poems but mostly I'm writing these letters to you, Lili. It's not like I believe Ms. Cooper—it's just that she made me feel a little stupid for thinking I was really a poet. I hate that feeling. And plus, the very next day after she said that, I got a forty-two on the pop quiz she gave us. It became just like in the olden days, before Ms. Marcus said I was a poet. Back when I used to get bad grades all the time. And then, after Ms. Marcus told me I was a poet, it was like my schoolwork started getting easy. Well maybe not *easy* easy, but if I got good grades and stuff, Ms. Marcus would let me have free time to write and that made me want to get good grades. But now Ms. Cooper and her mean old words and her big old belly are leaving. We're getting a new teacher. I don't know who it's going to be, but anybody is better than her. When she told us she was leaving, I wanted to stand up in my chair and start cheering. But I knew if I did that, she'd put a mark in the book by my name and I already have enough marks in her book. I hope her book leaves with her.

I got my fingers crossed that Ms. Cooper's replacement is going to be somebody who doesn't think you need a whole published book to be a poet!

Love,

x-poet
Locomotion